SPED-BOT

DroidMesh Trilogy Book 1

A Novel
by
Billy DeCarlo

Wild Lake Press, Inc.

Wilmington, DE

Copyright © 2018 by **Billy DeCarlo**

All rights reserved. No part of this publication may be reproduced, distributed or transmitted in any form or by any means, without prior written permission.

Wild Lake Press, Inc
P.O. Box 7045
Hackettstown, NJ 07840
billydecarlo.com

Publisher's Note: This is a work of fiction. Names, characters, places, and incidents are a product of the author's imagination. Locales and public names are sometimes used for atmospheric purposes. Any resemblance to actual people, living or dead, or to businesses, companies, events, institutions, or locales is completely coincidental.

SPED-BOT/ Billy DeCarlo. -- 1st ed.
ISBN 978-1732066915
LCCN 2018905321

Sign up for the newsletter at billydecarlo.com to stay informed about progress and release dates for new books, audiobooks, and other news.

Previews of upcoming works and short stories by Billy DeCarlo at Patreon.com/billydecarlo.

Other books by Billy DeCarlo:
https://www.billydecarlo.com/index.php/books

To parents, who only want the best for their kids

and

for Tasha.

"It's a father's duty to give his sons a fine chance."

—GEORGE ELIOT

CONTENTS

1 My Brother

ISAAC'S MOOD CHANGED; it seemed to become as cloudy as the overcast olive sky above. His father and his gynoid companion, sitting on either side of him, both sensed it.

"It'll be okay, Isaac," his father said. "He'll be fine." Harley ran his fingers through his son's bristled hair and noticed that Carrie had taken his hand to comfort him.

They sat with a group of others overlooking a synthetic sports field, all contained under a massive transparent dome. They were members of a small community—all that was left of a once-thriving species on a far-away marbled blue planet.

Teenage boys from two local schools were on the field, engaged in the sport of soccer. It was one of the few customs from the Old World that they had maintained.

Harley looked over Isaac's head and examined the female android, his most masterful achievement as a robotic scientist, built for his son out of both guilt and love.

Carrie was the first. Beautiful. Almost indistinguishable from a human.

The mandatory identifying traits still bothered him. The Leadership Council wouldn't go along with covering their cranial domes with hair. They wouldn't permit any degree of human emotion in their firmware, either.

"My new brother. My new brother," Isaac said with concern.

The gynoid squeezed the boy's hand. "Isaac," she said, "my analysis of the play indicates that Liam has most likely suffered a minor ankle sprain, and should be able to resume play. He isn't badly injured."

"Thank you, Carrie," Harley said.

"You're welcome, sir," she responded.

"My new brother," Isaac repeated. "He's hurt."

Liam sat up on the field. The spectators gave him light applause as he got to his feet, helped by his teammates. He limped in a circle and then broke into a slow jog to test his ankle.

"Way to tough it out, Liam," Harley shouted in encouragement.

The boy looked up at them, grinned, and then gave a thumbs-up to his coach before retaking his position.

The tallest member of the team, wearing a captain's armband, approached Liam and began shouting and motioning for him to get off the field.

"Get off if you're hurt, we're a goal behind, and we can't afford a gimp on the field." The boy's shouts carried up the hill.

"Ralph is bad. Ralph Sampson is bad," Isaac said.

"Yes, son. I know. It'll be okay," his father reassured him.

Liam looked toward the bench. His coach motioned for him to stay in the game. Ralph glared as they lined up for a corner kick.

The referee blew her whistle to continue play, and a teammate launched the ball toward Liam. Ralph cut in front to take the intended pass himself and dribbled toward the opponent's net.

Liam ran wide and parallel as the defenders on the opposing team closed in on Ralph.

"Pass to Liam, he's wide open!" the coach shouted.

Ralph ignored the command and continued toward the goal, winding up and firing a hard shot. The goalkeeper leaped sideways and deflected the ball away from the net. Liam had anticipated the outcome and positioned himself in the ball's path, booting it into the open goal.

"Tie game!" Isaac exclaimed. "My new brother Liam!"

All Liam's teammates except Ralph ran by to slap him on the back as they lined up to resume play.

"I calculate that with just over one minute left to play, and with the psychological momentum in our team's favor, there is a high probability of winning this contest," Carrie said.

The teams launched into motion as play continued. Ralph moved in and stole the ball from an opponent with a sliding tackle, then jumped up to take control. Another player beat him to it and sent a looping pass to Liam, who had gone streaking down the sideline, his long hair flowing behind him.

He looked to pass to a teammate, but a defender ran into the path. Liam feinted the pass, causing the defender to hesitate, and then took the resulting open lane. He deked again as he reached the goalkeeper, and eased the ball into the net.

"We win!" Isaac exclaimed joyfully. He pulled at his team jersey with pride. "Liam did it!"

"Yes, son," Harley said. "But remember, athletics are only permitted for recreation. We shouldn't get caught up in winning and losing. It's one of the things that caused the Breaking of the Old World, back on Earth."

Isaac looked confused.

Carrie simplified for him. "Winning is fun for a moment, but it is unimportant after that, Isaac. We mustn't take pleasure in the misfortune of others."

"Okay," he said. "Da, I want to play. Can I play on the team?"

Harley had known this was coming. It always did after they watched the games together. His heart dropped as he considered how essential it was to the son he loved so dearly, and how unlikely it was to ever happen. He mentally flagellated himself again for his decisions. *I shouldn't have allowed it. It isn't fair to him…*

His train of thought was interrupted by a slap on the back.

"Harley Harris," Ken Sampson said in a commanding voice. "Your new charge out there is a good player. Maybe talk to him about passing the ball."

Isaac shied at the sight of the big man and curled into Carrie's arms. The gynoid began to speak to him in a comforting voice, distracting him from the man he feared.

"Mr. Sampson…hello," Harley said. "Your boy Ralph had a fine game. Just fine. I'll speak to Liam. He's a good kid; he's just trying to fit in, being new in the school and all. Perhaps they play differently in the sector he's from."

Sampson scowled. "You better. The rest of the league will think you used the exchange student program for athletic purposes. That wasn't your intent in bringing him to live with you, was it? Because you know it's against the Code. We can't go back to the old ways.

"And we don't need you getting shipped off to the Seclusion Zone as punishment. In fact, I need you to step up your hours in the lab. You should be *there*, not sitting around here with the boy and his robot."

"We consider that term to be a slur, sir," Carrie said.

"Silence," Sampson commanded her.

Isaac burrowed his head deeper into her shoulder.

"I must concur with Carrie," Sampson's android companion said.

"You shut up too, Charles," Sampson barked. "Harris, I swear you gave me a defective robot."

Charles stepped back, almost seeming embarrassed by the comment. Carrie put a hand on his shoulder. *That's odd*, Harley thought. *They're not capable of emotion.* He made a mental note to check their logs when he was back in the Robotics Complex laboratory.

"It's just that it's the Day of Rest," Harley interjected, "and I haven't been able to spend much time with Isaac…"

Sampson scowled. "Carrie is more than capable of caring for Isaac and his…problems. That's what you built her for, right?"

Harley looked at Carrie, relieved to see that the gynoid was distracting Isaac from the conversation.

"Yes, Mr. Sampson, of course. By the way, I have some ideas for a few new projects to build on my DroidMesh platform. Can we discuss them tomorrow? I'd like to get approval and funding from the Robotics Council for the initial development and testing."

Sampson waved to his son on the field below. "Sure, I guess. Stop by and talk to me when we're back in the complex. I'm sure you're aware that I'm the likely choice to lead the council after old Bob Sinclair retires. I look forward to your support."

The players from both teams were dispersing below, and Liam began to limp up the hill to join them. Carrie pointed him out to Isaac, who immediately ran to him.

"Nice game, Liam," Harley said.

"Thanks, Mr. Harris," Liam responded.

"Just learn some team play, dork," a voice called.

They turned as Ralph and their classmate Kim reached the group.

"Ralph, Liam tried to pass," Kim said. "You saw what happened. It would've been stolen. He had a clear lane, what was he going to do?" She smiled at Liam. "Nice game, new kid."

"Thanks, Kim," Liam responded, looking at the ground.

"See you in school!" she chirped, trotting away.

"*Thanks, Kim,*" Ralph mocked him. "Learn your place, *new kid.*" He stepped forward and gave Liam a shove, knocking him off balance.

"Stop! Stop!" Isaac cried. He ran to Liam again and embraced him.

"Ralph, you played a good game. I tabulated your points, and they were the most out of all players…" Carrie began.

"Shut up, sped-bot. Take care of the little retard and mind your business," Ralph said.

"Isaac isn't retarded and doesn't require special education," Carrie corrected him. "I was created to help him understand the things that aren't clear. He has an intellectual disability.

"And technically, I'm a gynoid, the female gender…" she began to say before Harley silenced her with a gesture.

"That's enough, all of you. Ralph. Let's go," the elder Sampson said with a smirk.

Ralph turned toward Isaac. "My family helped build this world so there wouldn't be people like you. You were supposed to be canceled. Ask your daddy what happened to your mommy because of you."

Sampson grabbed his son by the collar, and they moved on, leaving Isaac sobbing. "I'm not a retard. I'm not."

"No, you're not, son. You're a better person than either of them," his father said, pulling him into an embrace.

Liam joined them and put his arm around Isaac. "Forget them, Isaac. Let's go home and play some virtual soccer, okay? We'll team up and take on anyone that challenges us. You're amazing at that. You can teach me some plays."

Isaac brightened immediately. "Really? Da, can I stay up late?"

"You sure can, son," Harley responded. He turned on his communicator and summoned his companion. "Betsy, call a ride for us. We're ready to go home."

A moment later a skycar appeared over the horizon and navigated the airlocks to enter the sports dome. It hovered silently for a moment before setting down on the ground next to them. The group boarded and took their seats as the restraint systems latched down around them.

They lifted off and made their way back through the airlocks to exit the dome. The skycar accelerated across the sparse terrain toward their home complex. Harley looked down at their world. Honeycombed compounds consisting of bubbled pods coated with solar collectors were clustered around yellow lakes. Purple mountains rose in a jagged line in the distance.

Androids clung to the outside of some of the domes, performing their cleaning routine. Other skycars whizzed through the toxic atmosphere along their routes.

"How was the game, Isaac?" Betsy asked from the vehicle's command seat. One of the setting suns glinted off her transparent cranial dome, illuminating the electronics within.

"Really great!" Isaac exclaimed. "We won, Liam won it."

"Yes, it was exciting, Betsy," Harley added. "Though Ken Sampson joined us at the end and ruined it somewhat. His son was also pretty rough on all of us."

Betsy paused before her response. "Mr. Harris, for three generations on this planet, your family has progressed your species in so many ways with genetic and android research," Betsy said. "Disease is nonexistent. We androids can't help much with human emotional traits, but can't you filter the negative ones out?"

Harley considered it, still gazing at the small remnant of human civilization below.

"The people who escaped here from the Breaking of the Old World were humbled by the near-extinction of our species," he said. "For three generations on this planet, we've been on our best behavior toward each other—happy to have survived and cognizant of the human behaviors that caused the Breaking. Perhaps we're starting to regress."

"I just did an analysis," Carrie said. "A primary factor is that those selected for the Migration from Earth were of good character."

"Except for the Sampson descendants, I'll bet," Harley said, laughing.

"Mr. Sampson is mean. Ralph is mean," Isaac muttered.

"Parents often pass their undesirable traits on to their children, Isaac," Carrie said. "Sometimes it's through genetics, sometimes by their example, sometimes through their teaching."

"Maybe I should try to introduce these traits into the genetic cleansing algorithms. Perhaps we can filter them out," Harley said. "Which reminds me, Betsy, we have to meet with Mr. Sampson tomorrow to discuss my new projects."

"Mr. Sampson is mean, Da," Isaac said. "He's mean to you."

"I know, son. But he's an influential member of our society. I need his support to get my projects approved."

The skycar carrying Mr. Sampson and his son passed them. Isaac became agitated when he noticed them.

"Betsy. Hit them. Run them over. I command," he suddenly barked.

"Master Isaac," Betsy responded, "I cannot harm a human. You know this. It's against the laws of robotics."

Harley patted his knee. "Son, you know violence is a horrible thing. It's not part of our world. I'm surprised…"

"Ralph is bad to me. Ralph is bad to me in school. Very bad. I don't like him," Isaac said, beginning to cry.

"Carrie, is this so?" Harley asked Isaac's companion.

"Yes, sir. I can confirm that this is the case." She held Isaac's hand, while Liam distracted him by talking about the strategy they would use during virtual soccer when they got home.

Harley looked again at the barren landscape of their planet as they flew over it, his mind reviewing a thousand possibilities. *I won't watch my son suffer. I'll find a way to make him whole…*

2 Sampson & Son

"T"AKE US HOME, Charles," Ken Sampson said to his android companion, seated in the command seat of their skycar.

"Yes, sir," Charles responded.

Sampson turned to his son. "You need to tone it down, Ralph. I know you don't like the new kid showing you up, but you can't always be the best. If there's too much trouble, the Leadership Council will shut the soccer program down. It was hard enough to get them to allow it."

"Liam and Isaac drive me crazy, Dad. They both get too much extra attention in school. That idiot Isaac always has to have his companion with him, whispering and explaining everything."

"He needs help, son. He's slow," Sampson said, dragging out the last word for emphasis.

"Why, though? Why is he here? He's the only one like that. We built a utopian society here on Novae Terrae by canceling the ones we couldn't genetically fix before they're born. Why did he get a pass? Because of his father? How did that happen?"

"The circumstances were unfortunate; apparently there was some error in the testing protocol at that time. At least, that's what Mr. Harris said. He's the foremost authority in this area. So, that made it much more difficult to deal with."

"Sounds to me like he got a pass, Dad. What if there are more kids born like that? We'll end up just like things were in the Old World—lots of defects walking around."

"It won't happen again, Ralph. We've taken preventative measures since then. And I'm going to petition the council to have the boy sterilized now that he's of age."

He regretted sharing the information with his son and worried that he might use it to further taunt Isaac.

"Don't you dare say a word," he added.

Sampson looked out over the landscape, broken up only by the domed complexes. The complete silence of the craft as it streaked over the terrain helped ease his anxiety.

He broke the silence, speaking more to himself than his son.

"I often wonder exactly what Harris is up to in that lab. With so much of our daily life recorded in distributed hyperledger logs and blanket video, it's hard to break the law without detection. But if there's one guy that could find a way around that, it's him. He's the lead architect."

"Mr. Harris is a good man. He created me and my android brethren," Charles spoke up.

"Shut up, Charles," Sampson commanded.

"You think he's up to something, Dad?" Ralph asked.

"I doubt it. Harris is timid. He knows he wouldn't do well in the Seclusion Zone without his kid. The boy is all he cares about since he lost his wife. He's been through a lot. We're no longer conditioned to deal with a lot of stress since we rarely encounter it."

"Well," Ralph said, "send Isaac and his dad to Seclusion and Liam back to wherever he came from, and the problem is solved!"

Sampson scoffed at the idea, and then considered it for a moment. "Harris and I played soccer together in school. We were rivals, much like you and Liam are now. I was the team captain, like you. Harley was nowhere near as good as me, though. In fact, he was kind of a dork.

"But what Harley lacked in athletics he made up for with his genius. He finished ahead of me, at the top of our class. He's scarily smart. I worry about that sometimes." *I wonder if I should be shutting his projects down, rather than advocating for them.*

"Well, you're his boss, just do it. But it sounds like someone else doesn't like getting shown up," Ralph said.

The vehicle remained silent again.

"Shall I play some music?" Charles asked.

"No, Charles," Sampson responded.

Ralph jumped up in his seat. "I see one!" His sudden exclamation startled his father.

"*Please* don't do that. You do that every trip. The underworld beings simply don't exist, Ralph. It's just a myth. If they existed, we'd know by now."

"I swear I saw one. It was moving fast, went behind that bluff."

"Son, when we're moving at this speed, along with other skycars in the area, it disturbs the surface dust. It causes mirages."

Ralph leaned forward and shook his father's shoulder. "I saw it, Dad. They're real."

"Alright then, let's settle it. Androids cannot lie. Charles, was there a life form on the terrain?"

"No, sir," Charles responded. "I have run an analysis on the object that Ralph saw. May I display it?"

"Of course, you idiot," Sampson said.

A holographic three-dimensional video began to play in front of them. A figure appeared on the horizon, framed and magnified by Charles' analytic interpretation module. As the video zoomed in, it showed a twister of surface dust, moving with the wind. The tracking frame followed it until it dissipated.

"Good eye, though, son," Ken said. "I didn't even catch it. Alright, Charles, turn it off before you crash the skycar."

"But they're real," Ralph said. "That's why I need a companion, for protection. Why can't I have one? The retard has one. So does his dad. You have one."

"Harley invented them. His son has a disability. You don't have an argument there, sorry. You'll have to finish school and work your way up through the Castes like everyone else until you're at a level where a companion is included. That should be sufficient motivation for you to study hard and work hard. That's how our system works."

Ralph slumped back, defeated. "I think I would have liked the Old World better. Kids like me could just take advantage of their parents' success and start at the top, rather than the bottom. Why can't we just have money to buy things, like they did?"

"Because money caused most of their problems. Particularly because the people at the top, those born into wealth, didn't know what it was like to struggle." Sampson paused to think. "But sometimes I think I might have liked it better as well."

3 Checkers

ISAAC CLAPPED HIS HANDS TOGETHER after jumping two of Liam's pieces on the holographic checkerboard. "Your move, Liam!" he said, leaning back to rest on Carrie.

Liam hunched forward from his seat on the floor and studied the board.

"I think you have me pretty boxed in, Isaac." As he looked down, a lock of his long hair fell forward. He pushed it back behind his ear.

"I'm gonna win, Liam. I'm gonna win. Watch out for me," Isaac said. He shifted impatiently, waiting for his turn.

"Are we brothers, Liam?" he asked.

Liam looked up from the board and paused for a moment. "We're like brothers. So yes, Isaac. We're brothers."

"Ralph was bad to you. Why didn't you fight back when he pushed you?"

Liam hesitated again. "I can't..."

Carrie broke in. "Isaac, fighting is forbidden in this world. It's a thing of the Old World. The hostility of humans toward each other was a large part of what caused the Breaking."

"Ralph is bad. I'll beat him up. Mr. Sampson is bad," Isaac muttered. He brightened and looked up at Liam. "Kim is nice! I really like Kim. She's nice to me."

"She is really nice," Liam agreed. He went back to studying the board.

Isaac leaned back on his elbows and looked up through the dome above them. "She's pretty. Maybe she can be my girlfriend someday. She's pretty and nice to me. Do you have a girlfriend, Liam?"

"No. We're only fifteen, Isaac. Lots of kids don't have girlfriends or boyfriends at our age."

"Someday I want to have a girlfriend, and I want to play soccer." He sat back up. "For real, Liam, like you."

"You will, Isaac. I'll help you, you'll see."

"Carrie, do you have a boyfriend?" Isaac asked.

"Androids are not programmed for emotion, Isaac," she responded. "We aren't like humans. We don't understand human emotions, as we've never experienced them. They are a mystery to us. We aren't permitted to socialize or communicate with each other privately. It's against the laws of robotics."

Isaac struggled to understand her words. "You'll find a boyfriend, Carrie," Isaac said. "I'll help you, you'll see."

Liam looked down at the board again, studying it intently, and the same lock of hair fell down and across his face. Isaac reached to tuck it back for him, but Liam flinched, jerking back and replacing it himself.

"What's wrong?" Isaac asked.

"Nothing," Liam answered. He quickly moved his last remaining piece, and Isaac took the opportunity to jump it.

"I win! I win, Liam!" Isaac stood and raised his hands above his head in triumph.

"Just like at the soccer game, please be careful not to rejoice too much about winning, Isaac," Carrie said. "Each time someone wins, someone else loses. Learn from the experience and be humble."

"Great job, brother." Liam clapped him on the shoulder. Carrie gave Liam a sideways look.

"Great job, brother," Isaac said in return.

Carrie stood. "It's late, gentlemen. I highly suggest that you use the remaining time tonight to complete your school assignments and get ready for class tomorrow morning."

"I don't want to go to school tomorrow. I don't want to go ever," Isaac said.

Liam grabbed a soccer ball from the shelf. "We will, Carrie. Let's dribble a little first, Isaac. Then we'll do homework."

They took turns chasing each other around the large room, Isaac squealing with glee. Carrie joined them, and the three continued, laughing, until an errant kick from Isaac knocked over a lighting module. It crashed to the floor in pieces.

They stopped and looked at one another, and then laughed again. "I'll repair it in the lab after everyone has gone to sleep tonight. It will be our secret," Carrie said.

Isaac's smile turned into a frown, and he furrowed his brow. "Where's Da, Carrie? I wanted to say goodnight. I couldn't find him."

The gynoid paused before answering. "I saw your father earlier. He must be on the premises somewhere."

"Sometimes I can't find Da. I want to say goodnight."

"I'll search for him, Isaac. I'll make sure he comes by your pod. Goodnight, gentlemen."

"Goodnight, Carrie," they said in unison, before going back to their game.

4 Trick Shot

HARLEY ROSE as daylight breached the dome, and walked toward the cleansing pod. He passed Betsy, who was sitting in her DroidMesh station, recharging, updating her firmware, and recycling fluids.

"Good morning, Betsy," he greeted her.

"Good morning, sir. Rejuvenation is almost complete."

"I approved and released the newest firmware update late last night. It's minor. Take your time, I still have to clean up and dress."

He removed his clothing and passed through the cleansing pod slowly enough for it to allow for biomeasurement.

When he exited, Betsy was up and had selected his uniform for the day. "Sir, the pod data reports that you've gained three point two pounds this month, and your body fat percentage has increased. I'll schedule a physical regimen for each evening until you are back into conformance."

Harley sighed. "Not that I'll have time for that—particularly after Sampson and the Robotics Council approve my new projects."

"You're presumptuous," Betsy said as she began dressing.

Harley watched her, marveling at his work. As he viewed her naked form, he wondered if he had subconsciously designed her to look so much like Jessica. *Jess…I miss her.*

He found himself wondering whether he should reopen his petition to the Leadership Council to permit androids to serve as partner surrogates. *It would be good for Isaac; probably his only chance to know and enjoy love and a relationship.*

He admitted his own selfish motive as well, wanting companionship but not desiring to find a human replacement for his wife.

He recalled how the board had shot his first request down, citing the algorithms that matched humans for lifelong, blissful relationships. *That's what Jessica and I had. There'll be no such match for Isaac. Not in a world where everyone is attractive, every face and body perfect in its own unique way.*

He walked into the living area and found Isaac sitting on the floor, engrossed in virtual soccer. Carrie sat nearby, observing.

"Almost time to leave for school, son," Harley said.

"Okay, Da," Isaac answered. "I'm playing against Ralph. Tie game, Da. I'm tied with Ralph. He's really good, but he's mean to me."

Concerned about Isaac's opponent, Harley stopped to watch. He enjoyed his son's happiness and engagement with the game. *Isaac is such a natural at this, so brilliantly strategic. If he could only have his dream and play on the school's team.*

Harley watched as the teams lined up and Isaac's players prepared to execute a corner kick. At the last moment, Isaac switched the player who was ready to kick with another.

As the first player walked past the ball, Harley noticed him subtly move it with the side of his foot. The second player approached the ball and suddenly pushed it to a teammate, who had a better angle on the net and pounded it past the unprepared goalkeeper.

"What was that, you moron!" Ralph's voice boomed through the audio system.

Isaac laughed and high-fived his father. A banner appeared indicating that the play was under review. The referee trotted to the center of the field to make his announcement.

"After review, the first player did move the ball, putting it into play. The goal is good, and time has expired."

"See you in school, sped," Ralph said, abruptly dropping the connection.

"Nice work on the trick play, son."

"I want to play, Da. I want to play for real."

"I know, Isaac. I know. Someday, maybe. I love you. Where's Liam?"

Liam entered the room as if on cue.

"You guys ready?" Harley asked.

"I don't want to go, Da. Ralph's mad now. He's really mad at me. I want to be virtual today instead."

Harley considered the request. He remembered Carrie's report of what his son had been enduring and wondered if it would be any different with his avatar there in his place. Attending virtually from home, he would be subject to the same type of verbal abuse.

"Son, it's important to be there. Socialization is vital for our society."

Isaac began to rise, weeping softly.

Carrie interjected. "Sir, my algorithms indicate a better outcome if Isaac can attend virtually today. To date, his virtual attendance is low compared to last year."

Isaac looked at him hopefully.

"Alright then, I yield. Just today though, and make sure all the schoolwork is done and done well."

It warmed Harley's heart to see his son's joy reappear, and he knew he'd made the right decision. "Thank you, Carrie. Betsy, please head to the launch pod and configure a skycar with our route. Liam, go with her. I'll be there in a few minutes."

When they'd gone, he asked Isaac to go to his room and prepare for the day's lessons. Then he asked Carrie to replay the most recent incidents at school between Isaac and Ralph.

The video presented in the room. Harley watched with sadness as he saw Isaac continually humiliated. "Enough, Carrie."

He paced the room and then issued another order. "Carrie, suspend."

The gynoid went limp where she sat, and the electronics in her cranial dome dimmed into darkness.

Harley walked to Isaac's room and found him at his workstation, waiting for class to begin. On the video monitor, he saw Isaac's avatar, the legendary soccer star

Pelé, sitting in the classroom. He watched as Ralph walked by, paused to look, then scoffed and shook his head.

"Son, disconnect from the avatar for a moment and let's talk."

Isaac complied, and Pelé's form dissolved. Harley took a seat next to his son and took the boy's hands in his own.

"What is it you want most, son? Think hard and be honest with me."

Isaac thought for a moment, looking at the floor. He surprised his father with his quiet response.

"I want a girlfriend, like Kim. She's nice to me and pretty. I want a girlfriend, Da. Someone like her."

Harley was struck with profound sadness, having anticipated Isaac's typical response about playing soccer.

"Do you think there's someone for me, Da? I'm different. There are no girls like me."

He found himself unable to address his son's wish and regrouped. "There's someone for everyone, Isaac. You just have to be patient. What else do you wish for?"

"You know what else. I want to play. I want to play, Da. Play for real. On the team, like Liam."

"What if I could help you do that? I'm working on something, and I'm going to ask Mr. Sampson and the Leadership Council for approval. If they say okay, maybe we can try. It's an experiment, but it could be dangerous. We'll have to make the decision together when the time comes. I want you to think about it. If you're afraid, it's okay to stay the same as you are. I love you just how you are."

"Will I still be dumb, Da? Ralph said I'm dumb and ugly."

"You are neither. You're my beautiful boy. You're smart. Look at what you did in the virtual soccer game today. You outsmarted Ralph!"

Isaac smiled. "Okay. I'll think about it. I love you, Da."

"Good. It has to be our secret though, alright? Not even Carrie can know. Just between us, right?"

"Okay, Da."

"Good. I'm going to work now, Isaac. Be good and study hard."

Harley enjoyed the boy's broad smile as Pelé appeared again, seated in the classroom.

"Carrie, wake," he said as he walked through the living room on the way to the launch pod.

5 History Class

"WE'LL BEGIN NOW," the android instructor announced to the class.

From his monitor at home, Isaac looked around at the assembly of students. A few avatars sat in for those who were attending virtually. His Pelé avatar sat erect, in rapt attention. Ralph sat one seat behind. Fear surged through Isaac's body at the sight of his nemesis.

"We covered the Breaking of the Old World in our last lesson," the instructor continued. "Let's review. Again, some of this may be disturbing, but it's imperative that we learn from the past for a better future.

"In the twenty-first century on Earth, the fallacies that human civilization was operating upon began to bring about the end of that world. For thousands of years, humans' behavior was kept in check partly by fear of a supreme being or beings. That control began to erode as groups with different religious beliefs began to slaughter one another out of hatred. Those who society counted on most to be ethical slipped into widespread immorality—doctors, clergy, judges, politicians.

"As humans developed more sophisticated weapons, they were able to kill much more efficiently and across far greater distances. Human technology had surpassed its declining morality."

Terrifying images of war played behind the instructor—huge explosions, people dying horrible deaths, destroyed land and cities, military cemeteries with oceans of white crosses representing lives spent for oil, hatred, greed.

Isaac looked away, at Kim, who was seated next to Ralph. *Kim is nice. Kim is pretty. Kim is my friend.*

"The white European-based populations around the Earth saw their majority and financial control slip away. This was exacerbated at the tipping point when democratic countries were overtaken by hateful nationalists."

The images changed to white people on the march with flags and torches, some wearing white robes and hoods.

Isaac watched as Ralph opened his tablet and began sketching. He strained to see what Ralph was drawing, but he didn't have a clear view. *Ralph is bad. Ralph is bad. Ralph is mean.*

"Are you okay, Isaac?" Carrie asked.

"I'm okay, Carrie. I'm okay. I like school. Ralph is bad, Carrie."

"That's true, Isaac. Focus on the lesson, not Ralph. Eliminate him from your mind. Focus."

The instructor moved around the room. "At this time in the Old World's history, the planet itself was beginning to fail, due to increasing abuse by humans. Clean energy progress reverted back to damaging dependencies on fossil fuels. Much of this was driven by human greed."

The classroom images changed to beautiful landscapes being strip-mined, oil rigs and massive pipeline spills, trucks and factories belching smoke.

Isaac looked at Liam, seated next to his Pelé avatar. *Liam is good. Liam is my friend. Liam is my brother.* He checked again to see what Ralph had drawn. He zoomed in, and it came into focus. It was a drawing of Liam with a bow in his long hair, wearing a dress.

Ralph reached across the aisle and touched Kim's arm to get her attention, then showed her the drawing. He appeared annoyed when she just shook her head.

The instructor continued. "The coastal regions became uninhabitable, followed by the interior of each land mass." Images of tsunamis, hurricanes, and flooding appeared.

Isaac touched his console to direct his Pelé avatar to turn around, then opened his communication channel and said: "Stop, Ralph."

The class turned their attention toward Ralph, and the instructor made his way over to see what was happening. Isaac watched Ralph quickly delete the drawing.

"Is there a problem, Mr. Sampson?" the instructor asked.

"I don't know what's going on. The idiot's avatar just turned around and said something to me."

The instructor turned to Pelé. "Is there a problem, Isaac?"

"No," Isaac said through the channel.

"Good. Let's continue. As we discussed, as the Old World came to its end, our forebears executed their escape plan and came to this new world we call Novae Terrae. Now, who can tell me what primary factors caused the Breaking to occur? Isaac, do you know?"

Isaac became excited that he was called on and opened his channel. "People were bad. Bad people."

Ralph laughed out loud, and the class tittered. "What a dummy," he said.

"Ralph, that kind of remark is not permitted," the instructor warned him. "I will record your response in today's logs."

Isaac felt a flush of embarrassment and considered disconnecting from the class.

"Your answer was correct, Isaac," Carrie said. "You should not be upset."

Liam raised his hand. Isaac noticed Ralph drawing on the tablet again.

"Yes, Liam?" the instructor asked.

"Well…The Proving happened, the scientific proof that there was no supreme being. The ancient relics and stories were shown to be false. Then the Third World War began because they couldn't handle it."

"Excellent, Liam," the instructor said. "What else, class?"

Kim raised her hand, and the instructor acknowledged her. "At the same time, the climate changes on Earth began to wipe out large numbers of the population."

"Correct, Kim and Liam," the instructor said.

The two smiled at each other. Ralph noticed, and Isaac could see that he was angry about it, and was sketching faster.

"Much of the worst human behavior was driven by lust," the instructor added. A wave of nervous laughter came from the class.

"One of the improvements we've made has been to dial the human sex drive down via genetic modification. The act is now a conscious one that people take to show their love for their partners or to procreate, rather than something they are driven to do at all times and at all costs to themselves and others.

"With this context," the instructor continued, "the decisions that shaped our new society were made. No religion, money, weapons, wars, greed, capitalism, autocracy or other forms of human domination over other humans. We are much like the original native populations in the Old World."

Isaac tried to zoom in to see Ralph's sketch, but it was turned at an angle away from his camera.

The instructor continued. "One of the biggest reasons for the Breaking of the Old World was because the rich had no idea what it was like to be poor or to suffer. Now, everyone receives from our society based on their contribution, and has lived in and can choose the Caste level they are comfortable with."

"Ralph's doing something bad again, Carrie," Isaac said.

"Ignore him, Isaac. Listen to what the teacher is saying."

Isaac tried to divert his eyes away from Ralph and toward the teacher as he continued.

"The Caste system was devised so that everyone would know what it is like to live at each level of society. Each person can determine where they want to be based on what contribution they desire to make."

Ralph finished his sketch and again poked Kim. She looked at it, and Isaac could hear her say, "You're disgusting," through his avatar's microphone. This caught the instructor's attention.

"Mr. Sampson, what are you up to?" the instructor asked.

"I just drew a picture," Ralph said.

"I'd like to see it," the instructor responded.

"No…" Kim said, leaving her seat and grabbing for the tablet. At the same time, Ralph pushed a sensor to project his drawing to the front of the classroom. It was a cartoon of Isaac, naked and sitting on Carrie's lap, breastfeeding.

Isaac screamed, and the Pelé avatar dissipated into nothingness.

6 BrainMesh

HARLEY STOPPED to check his image in a reflector panel, straightening his uniform and adjusting his hair. He continued down the hall, pausing just before the entrance portal inscribed with Ken Sampson's name.

He heard the voice inside command him to enter. "Is this a good time, sir?" Harley asked, poking his head into the pod.

"Yes," Sampson said gruffly. "It's when I told you to show up, Harris. I swear, for a smart guy sometimes you're pretty dumb. Come in and sit down. I don't have all day."

Harley entered and took a seat. He waited as Sampson scrolled through reports, ignoring him.

Sampson finally looked up. "I'm sure you heard about what happened in the school yesterday. My boy is in Separation for a few days, because your son simply cannot control himself."

"But that's not what happened," Harley began.

Sampson cut him off. "I've said it before, and I'll say it again, Harris. I don't understand how this happened. You could have selected any traits you wanted for your child.

Your son's defect should have been discovered, and he should have been canceled."

"I won't listen to you talk about Isaac that way," Harley said, standing.

"Sit down, Harris. You got a pass when he was born. We know that. It was a 'mistake' that didn't get caught in the genetic review. Some of it was, I believe, sympathy because of what happened to your wife after he was born."

"Jessica," Harley sharply reminded him.

"Right. Jessica. In any event, I think Isaac should learn on his own, at home, with no avatar. He's disruptive, and it's not fair to the other kids. Ralph is the one sitting home now. He couldn't go on the class trip today."

Harley tried to summon the will to confront the man about his twisted view. "Mr. Sampson. Ralph is…"

"Enough on that subject, Harris. I have work to do. What's on your mind?" Sampson asked while continuing to review documents on his monitor.

"Well," Harley began. "I have some new ideas for the mesh project. DroidMesh is stable. The companions are a functioning part of our society and useful in many ways. They provide security and do work outside the domes, where we can't go. They integrate with our vehicles to transport us. They integrate into our homes. They take care of menial tasks and teach our kids."

Sampson continued to be distracted, and Harley wondered if he'd heard a word he'd said.

"Got it, Harris. You did a great job. You're the father of robots. Well, you and your father and grandfather. Get to the point."

"It's just…I think we can do a lot more. I have a theory that we can tap into our consciousness, our thinking, our entire brain function, and share that with the androids…"

"Good heavens!" Sampson said. He stopped what he was doing immediately and stared at Harley with his mouth agape.

"I call it BrainMesh," Harley continued. "Think of the possibilities. This would make the avatars look like museum technology. We could take over the androids physically. We could do more without putting our own bodies at risk. We'd actually be *inside* them."

"This sounds insane, Harris. I can think of so many ways that it could go horribly wrong."

"It would give those who have physical limitations a way to overcome them, sir."

"Ah!" Sampson exclaimed. "And so we get to the real point. This is about your kid, isn't it, Harris? *You* made that mistake. You can't undo it. He is what he is."

"No, Mr. Sampson. It's about advancing our science and our society. It's about moving forward."

Sampson rose and looked through the window. Clouds raced by an otherwise clear green sky at incredible speed. "How the hell would you do something like this, anyway?"

"I've been researching brain waves. I have a theory that they can be read and integrated, just like we use wireless networks. Everything is in the air. The environment on this planet, even though it's similar to Earth, seems to make it possible. The frequencies are faint, but they're present. I think I can tap into them using neural lace. It might even make telepathic communication between humans possible."

"How would you test it? We don't have many of the creatures from the Old World left. They haven't taken well to this planet. You certainly can't test on humans first."

"We have some of the primates left. I'd like to eventually use one. To get started, I've cloned the primate brain in my simulator; it's close enough, anyway."

"I had no idea you were doing that, Harris. Listen, I'm concerned about the lack of oversight into your lab and whatever you do in there all day. It's just you, your assistant…what's her name…"

"Susan Clarkson."

"Right, Susan, and your companion Betsy. You've done a lot for our society, Harris. But we survive and thrive on openness, oversight, and compliance. No more secrets like there were in the Old World.

"And we don't seem to have that with your lab. I get a lot of heat for it. The others on the Robotics Council have brought it up. We never know what you're up to. They've thought about placing a few other scientists in with you. Younger ones."

"Spies, you mean?" Harley said. His voice began to rise in a rare display of anger. "I don't need anyone in my way, slowing me down. You said it yourself: society owes me a lot. I don't deserve this."

"No one is above surveillance and oversight. No one should have anything to hide."

"Fine," Harley responded. "But I'd like to proceed with these new ideas."

"I'll take your ideas to the Robotics Council, Harris. I'll go to bat for you, but I can't promise anything. If by some miracle it gets beyond them, it will have to go to the Leadership Council for approval. This has potentially significant consequences for our society."

"Thank you," Harley responded in a meek voice.

"Now if you don't have anything else, I've got work to do. And I assume you do as well."

Harley rose and left the room. As he made his way back to his lab through the Robotics Complex, he became more and more doubtful that Sampson would follow through on his promise. *I may have to find a way to go further underground.*

7 Class Trip

A GROUP OF STUDENTS made their way through a small zoo, peering into habitats with hands cupped around their eyes.

"Are there underworld people here?" Isaac asked.

Some of the students snickered. "No, silly, they're not real," one turned to him and said.

Kim sensed Isaac's embarrassment and stuck up for him. "We don't know that. We've been so focused on survival we've barely explored this planet," she said.

"Well if they're real, we need to put them in the zoo so we can all check them out," the student said.

"If they're real, then this planet is their home, and perhaps it's us that should be in *their* zoo," Kim said defiantly.

The student scoffed and moved along with the instructor and the rest of the class.

Kim remained at the primate viewing window. Liam, Isaac, and Carrie stayed with her.

"They're so beautiful," she said. She placed her hand on the window, wishing she could enter the habitat.

"I like monkeys," Isaac said. "They're funny and friendly."

Liam placed his hand on the glass as well, and Kim moved hers slightly so that just the edges of their pinky fingers were touching. Liam withdrew his hand.

"Sometimes I wish we could visit the Old World," she said. "There were so many different lifeforms. It was such a beautiful place."

"There were lots of people like me there," Isaac said.

Kim put her arm around his shoulder. They all began to walk to catch up with the rest of the class.

"You can visit the Old World any time, using the simulator pods," Carrie interjected.

"It's not the same, Carrie," Kim said. "I'd just like to *be* there, for real. Before the Breaking, of course. When it was beautiful."

"Da says there were people like me on Earth. Lots of them," Isaac said. "I want to go too. There's nobody like me here. I'm different."

Kim took his hand as they walked. "You're beautiful, Isaac. You're human, the same as the rest of us. In fact, sometimes I think that now we're all *too* much alike. Being different is a good thing. You're special, Isaac."

"Really?" he asked, swinging her hand back and forth in an arc as they walked.

"Yes, really," she answered.

"Do you have a boyfriend, Kim?" Isaac asked her.

"Well…no…," she stammered. She looked at Liam, who avoided her gaze. "Not yet."

"What about Ralph?" he asked.

"We're kind of…just friends."

"I'm glad Ralph couldn't come today. He got in trouble. You're pretty, Kim. Really pretty."

"Thank you, Isaac. I wish everyone thought so." She looked at Liam again. They had reached the rest of the group, and he was listening to the instructor describe the multi-colored birds in the last enclosure. Kim dropped Isaac's hand and moved in closer for a look.

"Why can't they be free?" Isaac asked.

Carrie spoke to him softly, taking care not to interrupt the instructor or distract the rest of the class. "Because this world is not like the one they came from. Humans have adapted to the differences with technology, but these beings are more sensitive. They don't have places in this environment to find food, nest, or fly freely. We have to take care of them in these controlled environments, or they'll die."

"They look sad," Isaac said. "They want to fly away, like me."

8 Proposals

SUSAN SAT BACK in her lab station to digest what she had just heard.

"Harley, this sounds incredibly dangerous. Are you sure that Sampson and the Robotics Council are on board?"

Harley continued to move about the Robotics Complex lab, tinkering with various pieces of equipment. An android sat in a DroidMesh station, staring straight ahead.

Harley answered her without pausing in his work. "Sure, sure. I talked to Sampson earlier today. He's okay with it. He's going to go through the formalities to get the council's approval. But please don't discuss it. It's sensitive, as you understand. We don't want to panic people.

"We'll do our initial experiments using the computer-simulated virtual primate. If those work, we'll start using the real one." He stopped what he was doing and looked at her. "Can I trust you?"

"Of course, Harley." She looked past him to an enclosure containing a sleeping primate. "Their brains are similar to ours, but there are still differences."

"Both human and primate brains possess metacognition. That means higher-order thinking skills," Betsy chimed in.

Susan looked sideways at Harley's gynoid companion. "Yes, I know, Betsy. I'm a scientist."

"I'm sorry, Ms. Clarkson. I didn't mean to upset you," Betsy answered.

"I'm not upset." *Why am I talking to this robot?* "Harley, will you come here and sit down and talk to me? Just us?" she asked, glancing at the gynoid.

He stopped his work and joined her on the sofa. Betsy walked to the area and stood by attentively.

"Just us?" Susan repeated.

"Betsy," Harley asked. "Please begin shutting the lab down for the evening."

The gynoid went about her tasks, and Harley looked at Susan with anticipation.

She spoke, measuring her words. "Harley, you've been through a lot. Much more than anyone in this new world was ever supposed to endure."

"Yes, Susan. I know, and a lot of that is on me."

"Because you put it on yourself. Since Isaac was born, and you lost Jessica, you've done nothing but work and care for your son. There's more to life than that." She paused and put her hand on his knee. "It's been fourteen years, Harley."

"I know," he responded. "I count them."

"I'm not talking about your grief. I've been dedicated to you and your work for a long time."

"And I thank you," Harley answered. Her hand remained on his knee, and he sat stiffly, as if unsure what it meant.

"I don't want your thanks, Harley. I've been singularly focused on this work, too. Whatever this is, this new project, however dangerous as it is, I'm with you. You know that. I've never betrayed you. I'm dedicated and loyal."

"I've never said you were anything else. What's this about, Susan? Do you want me to recommend you to the board for a promotion? Your own lab?"

She stopped to look at him, wondering how a man so brilliant could be so clueless.

"Harley, I've never taken the time for a social life. I have my reasons. I enjoy my work. I enjoy working with you. And I like Isaac, very much."

He shifted uncomfortably, and she realized he was finally catching on.

"What I'm saying is that I'd like for us to be more than just colleagues. I like you, Harley. I ran our profiles through the partner evaluation algorithm. We're a good match. We'd be good together."

He was silent. Susan knew he was running all the possible outcomes of a relationship through his mind. *Every scenario.*

He placed his hand over hers. "Susan… I do get lonely. I…"

"Will there be anything else, sir?" Betsy interrupted, as she rounded the corner back into the break area.

Susan glared at her. *This gynoid can't be that naïve. They're smarter than that. If I didn't know better, I'd think she was jealous.*

Harley glanced from one of them to the other, as if unsure what to say.

"I've got to go, Harley," Susan said, getting to her feet. "Think about it. I'll be back tomorrow."

She left the area and paused to collect herself before going out through the complex. As she reached the exit portal, she thought she heard Harley command the gynoid to prepare the lab for more tests. *Strange, he just told her to shut it down.*

She considered going back but continued on her way.

9 Capable of Love

CARRIE AND ISAAC sat together in his pod, reviewing the playback of the day's lessons from school.

"When the teacher is talking about the Old World, and showing what happened, it scares me," Isaac said. "It looks like it was a scary place."

"It only became that way because humans lost control of it, Isaac. The ignorant and unethical bred faster than the intelligent and moral."

Isaac paused the playback. "Maybe it was because there were lots of people like me there. Da said there were lots of people like me in the Old World."

Carrie pulled him close and hugged him. "The people like you were the innocents, and one of the few groups who were not at fault, Isaac."

They continued their review of the lesson. The teacher described a world society that had crumbled in slow motion. Isaac tried to make sense of how it could happen.

"Why didn't someone stop it?" he asked.

"Some humans hoped for intervention from a wiser and more civilized alien society. That never happened. And then our forebears decided that *we* would become the wiser and more civilized alien society. That's when the plans were put in motion for the Selection and Migration to our new home here on Novae Terrae."

"They're all so skinny," Isaac observed.

"In the Old World, humans were dependent on animals for their food. When the animals started to die off, many humans died as well."

"They ate the animals?" Isaac's mood darkened further. "I don't want to watch anymore," he said.

"Alright. Enough history; let's switch to mathematics."

"Can we stop for a while?" Isaac asked. "I'm tired."

She discontinued the classroom replay and sat with him in silence.

"I want to know about my ma, Carrie."

"She loved you very much, and she was courageous."

"Where is she?"

"She's gone, Isaac. It's best not to talk about it with me. I'll let your father know that you're curious. He'll discuss it with you further."

"You're kind of like my ma now."

"I'm your companion, Isaac. In that way, I do some things that your mother would have done for you."

Isaac took comfort in her words and nuzzled closer to her. He liked the feel of her arms around him. He felt loved and protected.

"Do you love me, Carrie?"

When she didn't answer immediately, he broke free of her embrace and looked into her eyes, waiting.

"Isaac, I'm an android. I'm not human. We are incapable of emotion. It's part of our design."

Her response disappointed him, although he already knew it.

"However," she continued, "I'm sure that if I were capable of love, I would love you very much. You are a special and wonderful example of the human species."

Satisfied, he curled back up against her.

"I bet Da could make you understand love. He can do anything."

"Perhaps he could. He is a brilliant man. But it is forbidden by the laws of this society. We androids do not need human emotion to perform our responsibilities. It would make us less efficient, and disrupt our decision-making capabilities."

"I wish you could love. I wish you could love me, and I wish that Kim would love me."

"Kim can love you. She's not an android."

"But she doesn't. I love her, but she doesn't love me. Love feels good, but love hurts too. I wish I were an android. Then nobody could hurt me. I wouldn't know how it feels. Dad could reprogram me so I wouldn't be different. I could be smart. I wish I were an android, and you were a real person, Carrie."

"You're smart, Isaac. You're a good-looking young man, inside and outside. I cannot feel love, but I can see well. Well enough to know this."

He continued to imagine, in silence, his life as a normal person. He imagined Kim as his girlfriend, and how well he'd treat her. He imagined himself as the star of the soccer team, like Liam, and how he wouldn't put up with Ralph's bullying. Then he drifted off to sleep.

18 Strong Signals

HARLEY RUBBED HIS EYES and thought about his conversations with Ken and Susan. He lingered on Susan. *She's attractive, like everyone else, but there's something else about her. I never noticed because I was so in love with Jessica, and then focused on Isaac and my work after the accident.*

He considered Susan's proposal.

A relationship… I'm not sure I'm ready, but maybe it'll encourage Susan to help with the project…and not betray me when she learns the truth.

His thoughts turned to Isaac. He considered again the decisions he'd made in the past and the harm that they had caused to others. *To Jessica.* It motivated him to shake off his exhaustion and continue the work.

He looked up in frustration at his two subjects. The test android sat in his DroidMesh station, looking straight ahead. The simulated chimpanzee looked back at him from the computer screen.

Harley pushed away the temptation to go straight to the live primate in the next test cycle. He looked over at its covered enclosure.

It will be your turn soon, buddy, as soon as I figure this simulation out. I've got to move fast in case the council shuts me down.

Looking at another monitor, Harley scrolled down the list of parameters for his next experiment. His eyes blurred from the strain. He began to rub them again and felt a comforting hand on his shoulder.

"Eye drops, sir?" Betsy offered.

"Thanks, Betsy. My eyes are shot. It's been a long night. Please turn off any unnecessary lighting and equipment to cut down the glare."

He waited as she darkened the lab. "What do you think, Betsy? Where am I getting this wrong? Please feel free to criticize my approach."

He turned to face her while he waited for a response. The electronics in her cranial dome brightened; something that only happened when one of his creations was pushing its processing power to the maximum.

Finally, she turned to face him.

"According to my observations, you keep increasing the frequency strength, hoping for a connection. In fact, it's too strong. You have been moving further and further from your target. The signal is distorted too much for either subject to recognize and receive it."

Realization struck him like a thunderbolt. "Thank you, Betsy! You're amazing!"

He went back to work at a furious pace, immediately reducing the simulator's frequency level and then recalculating the other parameters.

After reviewing the settings several times, he paused and stared at the monitor. Betsy stood next to him, her hand still on his shoulder.

"Simulate," Harley instructed.

The displays jumped to life, showing waveform graphs. Harley turned his head from the monitors to the test android and back, again and again. He watched the lines flowing across the monitor and thought he saw something out of the corner of his eye.

Then it happened. The simulated primate and the android rose simultaneously. The simulated chimp became animated, calling out and scrambling around on all fours. The android did the same.

Harley watched in amazement. The test android now moved across its enclosure to examine some objects that were left inside. Meanwhile, the simulated chimpanzee remained still, concentrated on the android's movement. *Amazing,* Harley thought. *The primate has already learned how to take it over without having to move its own body.*

"You appear to have achieved some degree of success, sir," Betsy said.

"I sure have, Betsy. I sure have." He thought about the possibilities for Isaac, his excitement growing. "We're getting there. This is a big step."

"I have to caution you against going too far, sir. You don't have official approval for this project yet. You have already overstepped the bounds of preliminary research."

"I know that, Betsy. Thank you for the words of caution, but I can't wait forever for their bureaucracy and regulations. Isaac is suffering every day. I want to make his dreams come true."

"Sir, I would remind you of a similar time, when you allowed your initial success to push you beyond reason in your work, for Isaac..."

Harley swatted her hand from his shoulder and jumped up.

"Don't you ever bring that up again, Betsy. I know damn well what happened to Jessica, but it was because of *her*. She was insistent, and I was trying to be cautious. She was the one pushing me..."

"Stop the simulation," Harley commanded the lab equipment. He sat back in the lab chair, folded his arms onto the desk and put his head in them, sobbing. The elation of his sudden success was lost to grief over what he had done long ago.

~*~

A voice shook Harley from his slumber. He lifted his head from the table.

"Harley, I asked if you've been here all night."

He picked his head up and saw Susan standing over him in her lab coat. She looked fresh and smelled great. He could only imagine what he looked like and could detect the odor on himself of a man who hadn't cleansed in days.

"Uh, no. I couldn't sleep, so I came to the lab early..." He panicked, thinking his night's work was all still exposed, and then realized that the lab had been cleaned and shut down. He looked across the room at Betsy, and she gave him a knowing glance.

"I guess it all hit me at once and I crashed before I could even get started."

"Okay," Susan replied. "If that's your story. What's on the schedule for today?"

"Ah, well, we have to test the new DroidMesh firmware so that we can deliver it to the android population by next week. Sampson's been on my back about it. Can you set up for that? I'm going to go home, clean up, and get Isaac off to school. I'll be back soon."

"Sure thing," she said as she began initiating the equipment.

"Great. Betsy, please summon a skycar and set our destination. I'll be up in a few minutes."

The gynoid complied, leaving Harley and Susan alone.

"Hey," Harley began. "About yesterday…"

"It's okay," Susan interrupted. "Forget about it."

"No, I was thinking. I mean, I've never been forward with women. I just don't seem to know how, and I always end up embarrassing myself. It's why I don't bother."

"Because you're a nerd, Harley. A brilliant nerd."

They both laughed, and it broke the tension.

"Let me be forward for you," Susan added. "How about we have dinner sometime soon? Then maybe go to a performance?"

"I'd love it," Harley said. "I'd hug you, but, um…" He feigned sniffing at his armpits.

"Yeah, I kind of know," she said, laughing. "You could use the cleansing pod here in the lab."

"No, I have to get back to Isaac and see him off. I'll be back, though." He left the lab, now elated by the prior night's success and the prospect of a date.

11 Kim's Game

KIM WIPED THE SWEAT from her brow and glanced up at the hill above the field. Isaac, Liam, and Carrie smiled and waved. Ralph sat alone a short distance from them. The other girls on the field took their positions.

"Pay attention!" Ralph shouted.

She took a moment to decide where she would place the penalty shot, and then strode toward the ball. As soon as her foot made contact, she knew that she had miscalculated. The ball sailed over the net.

"Oh, man!" Ralph exclaimed. "Hit the net, Kim."

She put her head down and trotted back to midfield. She could hear Isaac telling her it was alright. *I'd like to leave the field and just go sit with them. Relax and have fun.*

She played on until the game mercifully ended, then gathered her things as Ralph approached.

"Let's stay back and work on that penalty kick after the others are gone," he said. "Your team could've won it if you'd buried that."

She spun and faced him while she still had the courage.

"No, Ralph. No. I don't want to play anymore. It isn't fun. I just want to hang out—be a regular kid for a while."

He stood back with his arms up, palms facing her. "Whoa. Okay, fine. Let's just go to my house and hang out."

She felt stronger now, bolstered by speaking freely to him.

"I think I'm going to take a pass today, Ralph. I just want to go home and rest. I'm tired."

He scowled at her and stormed off without a word.

She felt lighter immediately. *Free.* She waited until she saw Ralph leave in a skycar and then began climbing the hill.

"Great game, Kim!" Isaac exclaimed.

"Good one. You're really good, Kim," Liam added.

They both greeted her with a hug—Isaac's a warm and prolonged embrace, and Liam's stiff, awkward, and quick.

As he pulled away, her hand grazed his long, soft hair. She reached to touch it again.

"I love your hair, Liam," she said. "It's so soft."

He pulled back reflexively. "Thanks," he said. "I was gonna get it cut."

"Don't!" she said. "It's different. Nobody is different around here except you two. That's why I like to be around you both so much."

Isaac rubbed his short, spiky hair. "I'm gonna grow long hair like Liam," he added.

They all laughed at the comment.

"Don't do it, Isaac," Kim said. "You're perfect just the way you are."

Isaac's expression broke the mood, as his smile faded and he looked at the ground. "No, I'm not. I can't play soccer like you and Liam."

"No way!" Kim and Liam said at the same time.

Kim continued. "You're handsome and smart, and you can play soccer, Isaac. You're way smarter about soccer than either Liam or me. You dominate on virtual soccer!"

Isaac's face brightened. "But it's not the same as real soccer. I want to play for real," he said.

"Then let's do it!" Liam shouted. He grabbed the ball from under Kim's arm and rushed down to the field. Isaac and Kim followed quickly behind.

"Come on, Carrie," Isaac called. "Two against two!"

The four of them ran about the field, switching sides, not caring about winning or losing. Isaac ran happily, calling for the ball.

The others adjusted their pace and passed to him again and again when he was in scoring position. Each time he pushed it over the goal line he called "Pelé scores!" in triumph.

Finally, they collapsed and lay on their backs, spent. As they caught their breath, they looked up at the olive sky and the bright suns shining through the cloud cover.

"Back on Earth, in the Old World, the sky was so blue," Kim said.

"It's true," Carrie responded. "Because of the atmosphere there, and the way the light waves bend, it was blue. Things are different here. We have a green sky."

"I think I'd like blue better," Liam said. "I bet it was pretty."

Isaac stood. "I have to go to the bathroom," he said. He went off toward the clubhouse with Carrie.

Kim found herself alone with Liam, lying side by side with him in the synthetic grass. Adrenaline coursed through her, and she found herself at a loss for words.

She reached over and took his hand, waiting for him to pull away, but he didn't. It felt slightly cool. The setting suns made her realize with regret that they would have to leave soon. "Do you miss where you're from?" she asked him.

"What do you mean?" he asked, sounding confused.

"The sector that you came from, Liam. Do you miss it? Your friends and your family there?"

"Uh, yeah. I guess I do. But it's nice here. I like it here too. Everyone's nice. Except for Ralph."

"I know. Ralph's different from everyone else. I thought I could change him, but now I don't think so. It's just a part of who he is."

Her heart beat faster as she summoned the courage to say how she felt about him. "I like you, Liam. I'm not going to be friends with Ralph anymore. I like you. You're quiet and mysterious."

He laughed at the comment but didn't respond further. Kim wondered if it was his shyness, or if maybe he just didn't like her. *Or…something else…*

She thought about how she had never seen him in the company of the other girls, despite their many fawning attempts to gain his attention. He seemed to keep to himself, and the only classmates she had seen him speak to were the guys.

Her conclusion gave her some sense of relief. *I hadn't considered that Liam might be gay.*

She recovered her earlier mood. "Come on, Liam. Let's meet Isaac and Carrie when they come out, and head home. I'll ride with you guys if it's alright."

"Sure thing, Kim. Oh, and I think you're pretty. And smart. And fun."

She smiled at him. "Race you!" she shouted, and they took off running toward the clubhouse.

12 Date Night

HARLEY SETTLED onto a lounge in Susan's home complex, nervous to be alone with her somewhere other than the familiar lab environment.

She handed him a tablet. The screen displayed all Harley's favorite dishes. He chose the cheese ravioli, then glanced at Susan, who was still deciding.

Looking around the room while he waited, he thought about similar nights when he first started dating Jessica. *So long ago.* He remembered their first date—how awkward he was, and how her confident strength and sense of humor had put him at ease. *Jessica...*

"Harley?"

Susan's voice yanked him back to the present. "I'm sorry," he said. "I was just admiring your home. It's quite nice. So, what did you order?"

"Thank you," she said with a skeptical look. "I went with the cheese ravioli. It's my favorite."

Harley felt a bit more comfortable. "You'll never guess what I ordered."

"The ravioli?"

He nodded, and they shared a laugh. "Well, you said that the algorithms had placed us as compatible. And as we know, the algos never fail, Susan."

"I love to jog when I'm not working, do you?" she asked.

"Um, no," he said. "Take off one point for the algos."

"The Human Relations lab programmers are good, but I don't think I'd like working there. I'm much more comfortable with Robotics. I guess you and I are alike that way, too."

A soft chime sounded, and she rose from the table to retrieve their meals from the food printer. She placed their steaming plates on the dining table and went back for the large glasses of wine.

"It's incredible how well the folks in the Sustenance Lab can reproduce the food they used to eat in the Old World," Susan said.

"The thing is," Harley answered, "how do we know this stuff tastes even remotely like it did back then?"

Susan laughed again. "Good point. There's the scientist in you, Harley. It's always on. Anyway, I like it." She took a sip from her glass. "And I like the wine as well. Sometimes I wish it still had just a little of the intoxicating effect it did back there."

"That would be scary. Alcohol was responsible for a great deal of the horrible things people did to one another in that world."

His comment took some of the lightness from their conversation. They picked at their food, glancing at each other.

"Is it okay to talk shop?" she asked, breaking the awkward silence.

Harley looked up, relieved. "I don't see how we could avoid it."

She laughed. He found himself noticing things about her that he never had before, now that they were looking at each other, rather than side by side staring at consoles. *A pretty, impish smile. Full lips. A small mole just above her lip. Eyes that twinkle.*

He imagined kissing her, then shook himself out of his fantasy. "I'm sorry, Susan. I was lost in thought. What was it you asked?"

"BrainMesh. When do you want to continue the work?"

"Well, we have a review with the Robotics Council tomorrow. If we get approval, I'd like to get right to it."

"I think they'll go along. Your record speaks for itself, Harley. This would be an important step forward for our society."

He felt his mood darken at the thought of facing the council.

"I'm worried about Sampson. He sort of gave his blessing and said he'd request this council review, but I can't help but think it's just a setup, and he's going to grill me to make himself look good."

Susan moved her chair closer, and her voice took on a sympathetic tone.

"I can see him doing that, but we'll be ready for him. Let's move into the entertainment pod and go over our points one by one until we have them down pat."

He preferred to stay at the table with a safe distance between them, and became apprehensive as she walked to the other pod. *I don't know how to do this...*

They sat next to one another on a large sofa that seemed to embrace them. She kicked off her shoes and laid back into an almost prone position.

"Play a romantic comedy," she instructed the entertainment system.

Harley tried to edge slightly away from her as he situated himself. As the movie began, his guilt and conscience interrupted again. *Jessica...*

"Oh, I love this one," she said, clapping her hands together. "Have you seen it, Harley?"

He focused on the movie for a moment. "Uh, no. Actually, I haven't watched a movie in years."

"How did I know that," she said, smiling at him. "Well, it's great. Let's relax and check it out while we prepare for tomorrow. C'mon, you seem tense. Tomorrow will be fine, we'll nail it. Lay back and relax." She pushed him back into the cushions with a laugh.

Caught off-guard by her shove, he sank backward. It felt good, and he didn't try to sit back up.

"Better, right?" she asked.

"Yeah, I guess so."

She settled in alongside him, and they began to watch the actors' holographs fill the room as the story started. He found himself laughing along with her. She slapped his leg after a funny line by the male lead and then left her hand there.

Harley wasn't sure what to do. He'd just begun combing through excuses to leave when she took his hand. He didn't move or release it; it felt nice.

He began to get comfortable, her hand in his, laughing together, when she turned on her side, facing him. He felt her gaze on him and ignored it.

She raised herself up on one arm, leaned over, and kissed him. He froze at first; then, feeling the warmth of her lips on his, he began to kiss her back. The thought of the lips he had been admiring upon his own thrilled him, and he put his other hand on her waist.

She pressed in harder and cupped his face with her hand. Suddenly he stopped and pulled away.

"What is it?" she asked.

"Susan...you're beautiful, and I like you very much. It's just, I still feel conflicted..."

"Jessica?" she asked. He could tell she was frustrated.

He immediately regretted his action. He wanted the mood back and wasn't sure what to say or do next. Susan waited, still looking at him.

"It's just...I still feel guilty. I feel like I have to save space for her in my heart, just in case..."

"What? In case *what*, Harley? What do you mean?"

"Well, if she comes back," he stammered.

"Comes back from where?"

He realized he shouldn't have responded. He began to panic. "I...I don't know...wherever they go." He paused while she stared at him in confusion. "It's incredible that with all we've learned, that's one mystery we haven't solved yet..."

Her voice softened. "Harley, she's gone. She can't come back. You have to accept that and move on—for you, and for Isaac."

"Speaking of Isaac," he said, looking down at his communicator. He tapped it, and the movie paused as the boy's image appeared before them, with Carrie in the background.

"Hi, Da," he said. "I can't see you, turn on your video."

"I can't right now, Isaac. Let's just talk. What do you need?"

"You said we were gonna play virtual soccer when you got home. I'm getting tired. Are you coming home?"

"Yes, Isaac. I'll be home shortly. Please be patient."

"Okay, Da."

Harley disconnected the feed and looked at her. They were both sitting up now, and the actors in the movie were frozen before them.

"Susan, I'm sorry."

"It's okay, Harley. I understand. I had a nice time. It's a first step. I know how difficult things have been for you. You have problems that we only associate with the Old World—it must be hard to handle."

He could sense her disappointment and felt torn between going to his son and trying to resume the evening he had only just started to allow himself to enjoy. He realized it would be futile to try to get the mood back and rose to leave.

As he reached the exit portal, he turned to her.

"Susan?"

"Yes, Harley?" She got up and walked over to him.

"This is all awkward for me, but please don't misinterpret that. Thank you for being patient. I had a nice time, and I'd like to do this again."

She smiled and leaned in to kiss him goodbye. "Sure thing. See you at work tomorrow. Don't sweat it; you and I are a good team, Harley Harris."

He smiled back and turned to leave as the pod exit opened.

13 Robotics Council

THE MEMBERS of the Robotics Council looked down at Harley from their horseshoe-shaped podium. He sat at a table below, facing them, with Susan at his side.

"Let me understand this, Mr. Harris," Mr. Sinclair, the council leader said. "You want to interconnect android and human brains?"

"Well, yes…" Harley began to respond.

"What could possibly go wrong?" Ken Sampson said sarcastically. Several council members laughed at the remark.

Harley began to sweat. The room seemed warm. He questioned again whether Sampson had set the meeting up to humiliate him.

"Stay calm. Don't let them goad you," Susan reminded him.

"It will be a one-way mesh," Harley explained. "The android mind doesn't send anything to the human mind. The human essentially takes over the android's body remotely, and the android mind suspends.

"Think of the possibilities regarding any of the remaining dangerous work we do. Think about exploring places we haven't been able to, like the subterranean levels of this planet. There could be alien life there."

"And what happens when something bad occurs to the android while the human mind occupies it?" Sampson asked. "Have you thought of the possible mental trauma and other repercussions?"

Harley fidgeted in his chair, thinking of the disaster that had occurred long ago, in his earliest testing of the concept. "I have. The code is set up to anticipate that. The connection is broken in that case—instantly."

"Describe your plan for testing this project," a councilwoman asked from above.

"I'd start with the simulated primate that I've developed. All first-stage testing will be via simulation. It's a very accurate representation of the chimpanzee mind. I'd start by meshing that with one of my test androids via the lab network." He could feel Susan's gaze on him. He wondered if she knew how far he'd already come, without the council's approval.

"From there," Harley continued, "I'd proceed with the live primate. As living things don't have network endpoints built in, I would have to use a small transmitter/receiver device. If successful, I would petition this group for permission to seek a volunteer from the Seclusion Zone for limited, supervised human trials.

"Good heavens!" Sampson boomed. "You would empower one of the few criminals in our society with the brainpower and strength of one of these androids? How would we control them after that? It would be chaos! Chaos, I say!"

The rant caused a raft of murmuring among the other council members.

"Let Mr. Harris respond," Sinclair admonished them.

Harley tried to explain. "No...no. I would limit the android capabilities that are available to the human subject. The android would be in a electronic geofenced enclosure during testing..."

"Insanity!" Sampson cut him off.

The board cut their audio feeds to conference among themselves.

"This is ridiculous," Harley said to Susan. "Sampson set me up to discredit me."

"Give it a chance," she replied. "All we need is a majority vote." She squeezed his hand. "I think we have at least a sixty percent chance of getting approval."

Harley smiled at her. "You're ever the optimist, Susan. I like that."

Mr. Sinclair cleared his throat. "Mr. Harris, we acknowledge your contributions, as well as those of your father and your grandfather, who was one of the Originals. You are almost single-handedly responsible for the scientific progress we've made. Your android companions have made life here much easier."

"Thank you," Harley said.

"However, your projects have not been without consequences—particularly of late. You seem...distracted. Your firmware updates have shown defect levels that were never common before. We will confer and make our decision."

Harley and Susan sat through the prolonged discussion up on the dais. Sampson appeared to be campaigning against acceptance. He alternated between gesturing animatedly and sitting back with a scowl.

"I think we're down to around thirty percent," Susan said.

"There goes my optimist," Harley said, his head down. "This is futile. I should be home with Isaac. I'm not spending enough time with him lately. Too much work."

"Mr. Harris," Sinclair said through the audio feed. "You have been approved by a close vote to proceed on a limited basis."

"Thank you, sir!" Harley exclaimed.

"Against my will, I might add," Sampson said, leaning forward.

Sinclair continued. "You will limit your testing to simulated primates only. No live subjects. This will allow time for the Leadership Council to discuss the moral and ethical implications. You will return to us with a demonstration of your progress, and we will make a determination as to whether to proceed."

"I'd like to thank you for your support," Harley said to the council. "As I always have, I will strive to reward you for believing in me and my research." He looked directly at Sampson. "You will not be sorry."

He nodded to Susan, and they gathered their things to leave. *Screw you people*, he thought but restrained himself from saying it aloud.

14 Movie Dreams

KIM TURNED OVER in her bed restlessly. She struggled to fall back asleep, in the hopes of returning to the dream she'd been enjoying. The harder she tried, the less sleepy she felt.

The warm glow of the scene began to slip away, and she grasped for it in her mind. It had been about her and Liam, partnered and happy together. As the faint recollection faded away, she gave up trying to hold onto it and took a drink from the glass on her nightstand.

"Play a romantic Old World beach movie," she instructed. A movie began to project into the darkness of her pod. She paused it and changed the settings to superimpose her and Liam as the lead characters.

She settled back and watched the image of herself on a white-sand beach with him. They lay on a blanket under an umbrella with a cooler next to them. Other couples, families, and children were nearby. In the distance, a pier filled with amusement rides jutted out into the ocean.

They sat looking into each other's eyes. Liam's hair fell over his tanned shoulders, and he smiled at her, then rose, pulling her up by the hand. They ran to the sparkling blue water and waited while large white waves crested and crashed to shore. When a lull presented itself, they both ran giggling into the surf. She squealed as he pulled her under until they were both submerged, kissing beneath the water.

The pod announced that her mother was approaching, and she paused the movie.

"Allow Mother to enter," she instructed the pod.

Her mother walked in and sat on her bed. "Is everything okay, honey? I heard noise and wanted to make sure you were alright."

"Sure, Mom. Just trouble sleeping, I guess."

Her mother rubbed her leg and glanced at the frozen scene. "It was a beautiful place."

"I wish we could make this world look like that," Kim said. "I wish I could swim in an ocean, ski down a mountain, or hike a forest trail."

Kim looked at her mother's face. Despite her advanced age, it was smooth, with only a few tell-tale signs that stem-cell treatments were unable to erase.

"We're lucky to be alive, Kim. Such a small percentage of the Old World people were able to get away. We're fortunate to have the few traditions we brought with us from there, like the sport you play, even if Novae Terrae is rather bleak visually."

Her mother peered up through the dome thoughtfully. "Maybe your generation can change that. The Growing Labs are making progress in generating synthetic soil. We have all the seed samples the Originals brought with them. Until then, you're stuck with the Old World simulator pods and movies."

"It's not the same," Kim said, glancing at the beach scene, herself and Liam still locked in an underwater kiss.

"Nothing is the same, nor will it ever be, honey. Novae Terrae is our home now. All we can do is learn the lessons of the past. It's not so bad, though. So, who's the young man you're kissing? Better play it forward before you both drown," her mother laughed.

Kim blushed. "Just a guy at school—Liam. He's a new exchange student, and he lives with the Harris family."

"He's cute. I love the hair, that's different. He reminds me of the hippies back in the Old World. Your great-great-grandmother Tara was one of them. They were young and idealistic as well. They fought for the environment, and for a fair society, free of hatred. If only they had succeeded."

"Yeah, Liam's different for sure," Kim said.

"Well, that's good. Sometimes I think we're too cookie-cutter in this society. The customs are different in the other sectors."

"I'm proud of you for being Isaac's friend, Kim. I sometimes worry that one quality we lack in our society is compassion. We have so little reason to use it, given our success in this new world."

Kim looked away and paused. "I'm not sure I'm always as nice to him as I should be, Mom. I think he likes me as more than a friend, and I'm not sure what to do or say, so sometimes I ignore him, and I don't feel good about it. I really like Liam."

"Just be kind and chose your words carefully, honey. Be Isaac's friend, but be careful never to give the wrong impression."

Kim enjoyed the opportunity to open up to her mother about the things that had been troubling her. "Ralph is still kind of insistent, but he's mean to Isaac, and Liam, and sometimes me."

Her mother smiled. "Good. I hate to say I told you so, but remember, the algorithms showed you two weren't a good match. Ah, to be young and idealistic. It's good that you kids still have a healthy skepticism of technology and get to learn some things for yourselves."

"Yeah, I guess so. I checked to see if Liam and I were a match, but something went wrong. I'm still waiting for an answer from the algorithms."

"They're always working the bugs out, honey. It's not exactly a critical system, compared to those that provide our life support. Liam's got to be better than Ralph, in any case. Bring him by for dinner sometime, to meet your father and me."

"I wish. Sometimes I think Liam likes me, but he seems…afraid or something. He could be gay, but why would he hide it?"

"Maybe he's just shy, honey. Nothing wrong with that. Customs may be different where he's from. Be patient. Give it time. Good things are worth waiting for."

"Thanks, Mom. I love you."

"I love you too, baby. Get some sleep."

Her mother kissed her before leaving.

Kim lay back and resumed the movie. She and Liam broke the surface, still in an embrace. She tingled with excitement as she rewound the scene to play it again in slow motion, zooming in on their faces and the love in their eyes.

In the movie, they walked out of the surf and back to their blanket, the sun glistening on their skin. They dried each other off with large, thick towels and sat back down. He pulled a couple of cold drinks from the cooler, and they quenched their thirst.

Pushing him down, she lay on top of him, brushing his hair out of his face and kissing him again.

She closed her eyes in the dark and tried to drift away, thinking about Liam and hoping for another dream.

15 Temptations

THE SIMULATED PRIMATE sat as if bored, while the test android waited in its DroidMesh station. Harley and Susan pored over test results in the brightly lit lab, looking for some hint as to why they weren't able to replicate the previous experiment's success.

"I'd just like to run some of this by Betsy," Harley said. "She picked up on the problems last time. I just don't know why we can't get back to where we were in my last tests with her."

Susan slid her chair next to him. "Let's give it a little more time first. I like it this way—just us humans. It's like the old days, two human scientists putting their brains together to solve a problem."

She rose from the chair and dimmed the harsh lights, then stood behind him, massaging his neck. "Sometimes you have to step back from a problem to *see* the problem. They used to say something about the forest and the trees, I think, when they had such things."

Harley admitted to himself that the massage felt good. Susan's hands kneaded deep into his muscles. He closed his eyes and leaned back to enjoy it and think. He was just beginning to review the test parameters in his head when he felt her lips on his. They were still warm and soft, and this time he didn't pull away. He kissed her back and felt her hair brush his face as they continued.

They broke off the kiss as she repositioned herself to sit on his lap, and then continued. Warmth spread through his body, awakening feelings in him that he had denied himself for a long time. *Since I lost Jess.* He pushed those thoughts away and wrapped his arms around Susan.

They sat together quietly for a while. Harley enjoyed the companionable silence and the weight of her in his lap.

"Alright, let's give it another try," he said. Susan got up, and he pushed his chair toward the lab console. After making some adjustments, he said, "Let's rerun it. Get everything ready."

"Okay, got it." She went to her workstation and began configuring the test.

Harley glanced up at the virtual monkey, and this time it seemed to look back with contempt. "You'll cooperate this time, simian!" he said.

"I told you it's good to take your mind off things," Susan teased.

"I feel good about this," he responded. "And that felt good, too…very good."

He smiled at her, his spirits buoyed, and his anticipation heightened. "Here we go, ready?"

"Kiss for good luck," she said, leaning over.

He pecked her on the lips then paused to smile at her again and turned to the console. "C'mon, work this time…" he whispered.

"Begin simulation," he commanded.

Script commands and log messages scrolled across the central console as waveform graphs danced across others.

The simulated chimpanzee blinked defiantly from a monitor.

"C'mon," Harley repeated.

Susan worked her side, looking like she was willing the experiment to succeed.

The chimpanzee stirred. Harley pushed in even farther, his gut mashed against the lip of the table, peering at the console messages.

>*Connection successful.*

The android opened his eyes and sat forward in his seat, looking around. "Ha!" Harley shouted. He thought of Isaac and what this could mean for his son, and it filled him with happiness. He grabbed Susan by the shoulder. "How about that?" He leaned over, and it was he who initiated the kiss this time.

Harley turned back to the monitors.

>*Connection failed.*

Harley, Susan, and the android all sat back simultaneously. The chimpanzee stared from its monitor, and the android's eyes slowly closed.

"I'm sorry…" she began.

"It's not your fault, Susan," he said with frustration.

"Let's try again, Harley.."

He stared at the test data in disbelief. "No. It's been a long day, Susan. Let's call it a night. I'm burnt out." They both worked at shutting down the equipment.

"Do you want to come over and relax?" she asked, returning her hand to his knee.

He stood. "Thanks, but I wouldn't be good company tonight. I'm going to go home, cleanse, and spend some time with Isaac before he has to go to bed. Maybe after he's asleep, I'll run some of these algorithms through the systems in my home lab."

She got up and gathered her things. "Alright. Don't take it too hard, Harley. Tomorrow's another day. We'll figure this out."

He looked at the enclosure that held the live chimpanzee. "I just think we're wasting our time with this stupid computer-simulated chimp. We're just appeasing Sampson and the council. We should get right to the live primate."

"Harley, we can't…"

"Don't tell me what I can or can't do, Susan," he shouted. He regretted the outburst instantly. "I'm sorry."

He moved closer to her, but she started to make her way to the exit.

She paused before leaving. "Harley, something I forgot to mention."

"What is it?"

"Sampson asked me to meet with him in his office tomorrow morning. I don't know what it's about. I'll be late to work."

"I can only imagine. Alright, take your time. Again, I'm sorry."

"I'll see you tomorrow, Harley."

She left, and he sat back down. He thought about Susan, and his heart ached. *I'm falling in love. After Jess's accident, I dedicated the rest of my life to Isaac. Now I'm getting distracted. It's not fair to me, it's not fair to Isaac, it's not fair to Susan. And it's not fair to Jessica.*

He made his decision and felt a renewed sense of purpose. "Betsy, awaken," he called.

She entered the room. "I'm glad you've finally called me, Harley."

"Me too. Let's power this equipment back up. And we'll be moving this project to my home lab. It's going to be just you and me working on it from now on."

"I think that's a good decision, sir," she said, going right to work.

16 Be My Girlfriend

THE IMAGE STARING BACK from the grooming station was not the one Isaac wished to see. He ran his fingers through his dark bristled hair. He wanted to see someone who looked like his classmates—attractive, maybe even with long hair like Liam.

"Why am I the only one who looks like this?" he asked the image. "Who am I? What am I?"

"Do you need help, Isaac?" Carrie called to him from outside the pod.

"No." *Why does everyone think I need help with the simplest things?*

He experimented with different hairstyles and clothing, from demure to radical. With every change, he still saw the same person looking back at him. Frustrated, he went back to his familiar appearance and exited.

"You look great today," Carrie said.

"I look the same. Same as every day," he said glumly.

"That's not true. You're growing. Growing into a fine young man."

"I'm the smallest one in my grade level. Ralph said I'm a runt."

"Come here, Isaac." She led him to a lounging area, and they sat together. "Look at me. I have an ugly head full of exposed electronics, not the beautiful hair that you humans have. But I'm smart and good at my job. I don't spend a moment thinking about what my head looks like, and neither should you."

"Well you don't have a boyfriend, and you can't have a boyfriend. Androids don't care what they look like. Humans are different. I wish I were an android. I'd rather look like you than me. I should be an android because I'm never gonna have a girlfriend."

"From what I know about the Old World, those who were different often made better partners because they were humbler. They were more appreciative than those who were more gifted and entitled. And that's how it will be for you. You will find the right one for you eventually. You're young. Be patient."

"I already know the right one. I love her, but she doesn't love me. I try to talk to her at school, but she doesn't listen. I try to video link her, but she doesn't answer."

"Well, keep trying, but know when to move on. If it's not to be, then perhaps there is someone else that you aren't considering because your attention is only on this one person. You're speaking of Kim, correct?"

"Yeah. Kim."

"She's a good girl, Isaac. I'm not really well-equipped to understand things like this and give advice but maybe try again with her. I do know that persistence is a good thing."

Isaac smoothed his uniform with his hands. "Where's my Da, Carrie? I couldn't find him when I woke up."

The gynoid took a moment before responding. "He's here in the home complex somewhere. Maybe in his lab…"

"I looked there. I looked all over. He's not here."

"I'm sure he is. I'll find him. Give your friend Kim a call."

"I will, Carrie. I'm gonna call her now. Can you leave?"

"Yes. Good luck. I'll be around if you need to talk more."

The gynoid left the area, and Isaac went back to the grooming pod and changed his hair again, choosing a part on the side and flipped-up front. He walked to his personal pod and sat down in front of the communication console. "Call Kim, please," he asked the system.

He waited for the attempt to time out, as it usually did. He watched the screen hopefully as the final seconds ticked down.

As he was about to get up, her holographic image appeared. She was sitting in her bedroom pod, at a pink vanity. The sight of her brought an immediate smile to his face, and he felt his heart flutter.

"Hi, Isaac!" she said.

"Hi, Kim! I'm glad you answered. I've been trying…"

"I know. I'm so sorry. I've been pretty busy with everything lately."

He let his excitement wash over him. He reached back to smooth his hair and sat up straight to make himself appear taller.

"So what's up?" she asked.

He felt himself blushing, and his mind clouded. He hadn't anticipated that she would answer and wasn't sure what to say. "I was… I was just calling you…"

She appeared to sense the awkwardness and filled the silence herself.

"I was just getting ready for school. Are you going today, or using your avatar?" Kim asked.

"I'm gonna go. I like going, except when Ralph is mean to me. I like going to see you because you're nice."

"Good! I like to see you too." She paused a moment as if to consider what she'd said. "I like to go and see everyone at school. Don't worry about Ralph."

"I won't," he replied.

There was another period of silence as they sat looking at each other. Isaac wished he could sit and watch her without talking. He pressed the capture sensor on his console to preserve the session and hoped she wouldn't know he had done so.

"Alright, well, I'm going to go finish getting ready. I'll see you in school, okay?"

"Okay," he said. He felt himself becoming anxious. He watched as she began to reach to disconnect their session. "Wait...Kim," he blurted out.

She turned back to him. "Yes, Isaac?"

"Would you be my girlfriend?" he asked.

Kim's expression changed. She looked uncomfortable, and he thought about disconnecting the session himself. His face flushed again, and he wished he hadn't taken Carrie's advice.

She seemed a little shocked by the question. Finally, she answered. "Isaac... I like you, but as a friend. Please don't get upset. You're nice, and I like having you as a friend. We have so much fun..."

He reached over, disconnected the session, and slumped back into his chair. Getting up, he went back to the grooming station and viewed himself again. *She didn't even notice my hair.*

While glaring at the image of himself, he mussed his hair and then yanked at it with both fists. He slapped himself hard on the face, then returned to his personal area and threw himself on the bed face-down, crying.

17 I Don't Belong

HARLEY FELT GUILTY for watching, but his love for his son wouldn't allow him to turn away.

As the conversation ended, his pride at seeing Isaac talking to the girl changed to heartbreak of his own. He knew what her answer would be, and he knew it would devastate his son. *Why did Carrie suggest this? Her algorithms should have pre-determined this outcome.*

He waited until the call ended, and gave his son a few moments before entering the room, motioning to Carrie and Betsy to remain behind. As the boy sobbed into the soft bedding, Harley paused to push the anger growing inside him away.

He placed a hand on Isaac's shoulder and sat on the bed.

"What's wrong, son?" he asked.

Isaac turned on his side and looked at his father with watery eyes. "I'm not going to school today. I don't belong here, Da. Why am I here?"

"None of us know why we're here, son. None of us are perfect. As far as we know, we only get one life, and it's up to us to make the most of it. When I was your age, I wanted to be a professional soccer player. I was angry that we don't have such a thing as professional sports in our new society. But I learned that it wasn't my destiny, it wasn't for me, and I found something that I love more."

"I can't even play soccer, Da. I can't play on the team."

"Well, I wasn't very good either." Harley felt a pang of regret. In his urgency to offer some comfort to Isaac, he had managed to hurt him all over again. His need to put his distressed son at ease made him think harder.

"When I was your age, there were girls I liked also, but they didn't like me in that way. I realized later that they weren't for me. Then I found the perfect woman—your mother."

Isaac perked up at the mention of his mother. "Really, Da?"

"Yes, Isaac. And when I got shot down, I was just as upset as you are now—every time." He laughed, and as he had hoped, the boy smiled as well.

"Isaac, in the Old World there were a lot of people who were different and challenged. What they learned was to let experiences like this motivate them to work harder, to try harder to achieve their goals. They channeled these bad experiences into strength. They learned that confidence and hard work can overcome not being as attractive or as good an athlete as those who are gifted."

It pleased him that Isaac seemed to be listening intently, and seemed to understand. His son embraced him, and the gesture filled Harley with love.

"Alright. I'm going to be spending more time working in the home lab, Isaac. It will allow us to spend more time together."

That brought another smile to his son's face. Harley rose again to leave the room.

"I don't want to go to school today, Da."

Harley considered the request. "I understand. Embarrassment is normal. You can send Pelé instead, but make sure you pay attention and complete all your assignments."

"Okay. I couldn't find you before. Where were you?"

Harley wished he had made it out of the pod before the question. "I was...I was in the cleansing pod, getting ready for work."

"I looked. You weren't there. I can't find you sometimes. Where do you go?"

Harley searched for an answer he hadn't already given. He didn't want to ruin the mood, and the progress he had made with his son, by lying again.

"I just have an alone place, Isaac. It's important to me to be by myself sometimes. I'll show it to you sometime when you're ready."

Isaac looked confused but got up as well. "Okay, Da."

Relieved, Harley hugged his son once more, then left the room in a hurry.

18 Luddite Vendetta

KEN SAMPSON STRAIGHTENED himself and addressed the members of the Leadership Council in his most sincere tone.

"We've worked hard to make this a pure society," Sampson said. "I don't see how we can allow it. We don't want to start making exceptions and slide down the same slippery slope they did in the Old World. We were supposed to be different."

He felt uncomfortable with the members of the council looking down at him. He wasn't used to being in a subordinate position, and he didn't like it.

"Mr. Sampson," Ms. Tillis, the council leader began. "What you propose is extreme. To sterilize the young man because he's different is something akin to the thought process that brought down the Old World."

The suggestion angered him, but he knew he had to suppress the emotion or risk losing his case. "No. I don't harbor that kind of intent. My concern is for Novae Terrae. Our almost-perfect world."

Another council member spoke up. "The boy is unlikely to find a partner, in any case."

Sampson saw an opening and conjured a compassionate tone. "That's what I mean. It was unfair to allow him to be born in the first place. We all know that he slipped through the testing phase. He should have been canceled then, or shortly after the mistake was discovered, when he was born. It was our mistake back then."

"Sir, you were aware at the time..." Charles whispered to him.

"Silence, you idiot," Sampson hissed while muting the audio feed.

"What is done is done," another member interjected. "The boy causes no harm to our society. Perhaps it's you who is at fault—you dislike him because he's different. That's a thing from the Old World. Remember, Mr. Sampson, the same can be said for your own son. Both boys were born around the same time. Your son also has certain traits ..."

"Don't compare Ralph to that—" Sampson blurted out. He stopped himself short of using the slur that would likely further anger the council.

Ms. Tillis spoke up. "Mr. Sampson, control yourself. Let me remind you that the boy's condition isn't hereditary. Your request is absurd in that light, and shall not be considered. This is our decision. Now let's move on to the other matter, which is of more importance."

Sampson composed himself. "Yes, this ridiculous BrainMesh project that Harris dreamed up. I have concerns."

"We are aware of the project and have read through the Robotics Council's proceedings," Ms. Tillis said. "Your concerns are expressed therein. It appears the council agreed to continue, but with some limitations."

"Yes," Sampson countered. "But that was from a robotics perspective. I've come before the Leadership Council to argue the ethical considerations."

"We have been discussing those, as is our purview. Our society has always had to make difficult decisions to survive here. Almost all those matters involved conflicts between technology and ethics."

"Yes," Sampson said. "Harris once wanted to allow the robots to be used as partner surrogates. I was happy to hear your decision on that matter. That kind of thing was part of the perversion of the Old World."

"Mr. Sampson," a member said. "It seems to us as if you have some kind of competitive vendetta against Mr. Harris."

"No, that's not it. That's not it at all…"

Ms. Tillis interrupted him. "Regardless, Mr. Sampson. We're curious about the benefits of the BrainMesh project. It has been limited to simulated testing so far. We consider that approach to be safe. It gives us time to consider the ethical and societal impact of the technology."

"But I don't trust Harris to stay within the guidelines…" Sampson tried to interject.

"In the meantime, we are thankful for your oversight of the project. That is what you can do for our society, Mr. Sampson. Conduct diligent oversight and ensure that things don't go astray."

"If we lose control of the androids…"

"We trust Mr. Harris' judgment and technical capabilities. He and his father before him have provided great benefit to our society through their work and research. You must put your competition with him aside,

Mr. Sampson. It makes you look like the lesser man." Ms. Tillis began to gather her things, signaling the rest of the council to do the same.

Sampson continued, frustrated. "He hasn't always been careful, though. We still don't know what happened to his wife. He said it was a heart attack. I don't believe it. Her disposal wasn't done by the protocol..."

"Conspiracy theories are a thing of the Old World, Mr. Sampson," one of them said firmly. "Water under the bridge, as they used to say when they had water and bridges."

The council members rose, signaling the end of the meeting.

Sampson remained silent, stewing as he watched them leave one by one.

"Charles, please prepare a skycar," he said to his companion.

On their ride home, Sampson spoke, more to himself than to Charles. "They've become blind. Too trusting. We're complacent now, our guard is down. We've had it too easy. They don't see the danger in Harris' project."

"I think Mr. Harris is a brilliant scientist. He created us," Charles chimed in.

"Shut up, Charles. Who's asking you, anyway? Whose side are you on?"

The android remained silent.

"Charles, I asked you a question."

"You ordered me to shut up, sir. And as an android, I cannot take sides. I can only present my interpretation of factual information."

"Oh, brother," Sampson sighed. He simmered for the rest of the trip, thinking of a way to interfere with Harris while staying within the rules.

As they were gliding in for a landing at his home complex, an idea came to him.

19 Interference

SUSAN WALKED the long hallway to Sampson's office. She reached the entrance and paused her communicator to avoid interruptions. The opening finally cleared, and she walked in, finding him sitting at his desk.

Clearing her throat, she took a seat, not waiting for him to offer. "I've got to get to the lab, Mr. Sampson. What is it you wanted to discuss?"

He looked at her. "Yes, Ms. Clarkson—the lab. As you know, I have oversight of the projects that you and Harris are conducting. I'd like an update."

She immediately suspected an ulterior motive for his question and took a moment to compose her response. "Things are progressing slowly. We are staying within the bounds established by the Robotics Council."

"I'd like more detail, Susan."

She couldn't suppress a deep sigh. "We had some initial success, but as we've tried to advance the capabilities, we've had setbacks. Something is interfering with the protocol communication. We've been unable to get back to our initial level of success."

"And why do you think that is?"

Susan pressed her lips together tightly, not wanting to provide Sampson with information. His patient stare forced her to give in. "Mr. Harris believes it's something in the code for the simulated primate. Don't you think that you should ask Mr. Harris these questions rather than myself?"

Sampson pushed himself back from the desk and placed his hands in his lap. "You're easier to talk to, Susan. You're also easier to look at."

She absorbed the shock she felt at his words. "What? That sounds like a remark from the Old World. What does that have to do with anything? You are partnered, Mr. Sampson."

"Take it easy, Susan. I was stating a simple fact. I'm a scientist, a man of observation."

She thought about how well-known his scientific shortcomings were in the community and held back a laugh. *I can't wait to let Harley know about this nonsense.*

"Are we done here, Mr. Sampson?"

He gazed at the barren landscape outside, dotted with human complexes, pale lakes, and clusters of vegetation. "I'd think an impatient scientist like Harris would get frustrated in that case and want to go right to the live primate."

"Are you doing surveillance, Mr. Sampson? Why would you say a thing like that? Mr. Harris has always been by the book. You know that."

"The fact that you ask me about surveillance could lead me to believe I'm correct."

"That's not the case," she responded quickly. "It's the fact that you asked."

"Do you feel that Mr. Harris is motivated to take risks incurred by this technology purely to 'fix' his son somehow?"

"That's a ridiculous question, Sampson." The look he gave her confirmed that they both knew she was lying, even if she hadn't admitted it to herself yet.

"Mr. Sampson," he corrected her.

"Apologies. Mr. Sampson. BrainMesh will lead to great benefits for our society. We laid our points out in the Robotics Council meeting. Think about it. It could bring telepathic communication and so much more."

She reminded herself not to allow her growing frustration and anger to cause her to say more than she wanted to.

"Are we through?" she asked.

"No, we're not. I understand that you and Mr. Harris have developed somewhat of a...personal relationship. Is that the case?"

She was momentarily embarrassed before becoming angry at his intrusion into her affairs. "I don't see how that's any of your business. Neither of us is partnered, and there are no rules against it. Again, I don't see how it's any of your concern."

He smiled at her. "Are you assisting him in his work at his home lab as well, or is he only working with his companion Betsy in those endeavors?"

He caught her by surprise again, playing with her emotions. "I...I don't think there's any work on this project being done there. He does some of the mundane work in the home lab—firmware updates, things like that. It's a much simpler environment than the Robotics Complex lab."

"Are you sure?" Sampson asked.

"Yes, I'm sure," she said. She began to wonder about Harley's recent behavior and whether Sampson could be right. She stood. "I've got to get to the lab. We've got a lot of work to do."

"Please keep me in the loop. Good luck." He smiled again, but then it changed into a sneer. "Oh, and I'd appreciate if you didn't share our conversation with Mr. Harris."

She turned and left, anxious to get back to work, and to Harley. *I can help Harley get past this snag, I know I can.*

As she made her way back down the hall, she enabled her communicator. A message from Harley popped up immediately. She paused to watch as his image appeared on the screen.

"Hi, Susan. I'm going get some things done in the home lab today. Maybe a break will help clear my mind. I hope your meeting with Mr. Sampson went well! Bye now."

28 Liam's Secret

IT WAS a Day of Rest, and Isaac immersed himself in the only world he felt comfortable in. He navigated his avatar on the virtual World Cup field, a gaming replication of the great soccer tournaments of the Old World.

He *was* Pelé, as the prodigy wove his way through defenders with time running out and the massive crowd roaring. Isaac felt his hero's physique through the simulator's full body suit. He felt his toned muscles rippled with every stride.

I'm Pelé. I'm the Great One.

He flew into an opening in the defense with smooth acceleration, feeling his cleats grab the soil and rocket him forward. The defenders, in a show of respect for his incredible skills, all converged on his path in an attempt to stop him. Using his keen peripheral vision, he spotted the resulting gaps that left his teammates open. Just as two defenders reached him from opposite sides, he popped a pass across the field.

As the defenders reacted and spread back out, Isaac made a beeline for the net. He could feel the sweat cooling on his jersey and rolling from his face in the wind. His teammate returned the pass with a perfect header.

As the ball arced through the air, he seemed to see it in slow-motion. His intuition and skill launched his body into action. He leaped into the air and executed his famous bicycle kick, arching his body backward and throwing his legs above his head.

He felt the arch of his foot impact the ball, and before he tumbled to the ground, he saw it fly toward the net like an inbound asteroid. As he landed in a heap on the turf and breathed in the fresh green grass and loamy soil, he heard the crowd erupt in a deafening roar.

His teammates buried him in a sweaty human pile.

As time expired and the virtual game came to a close, the crowd noise becoming distant, Isaac put his controller down and hung his head.

"That was amazing, son. You're a brilliant soccer strategist."

He turned to find his father standing behind him, watching. He jumped up and threw himself into his waiting arms.

"I was Pelé, Da. I won. Everybody loved me." He put his controller down and took off his headset. "Now I'm just Isaac."

"And Isaac is beautiful. I think Isaac is better than Pelé," his father comforted him.

"I don't feel beautiful, Da. I want to be normal. I want to play, like Liam."

"I know, son. I know. I'll help you, you'll see."

"I was Pelé, now I'm Isaac again. Just Isaac." He looked down at the control set and considered throwing it across the room.

He felt his father's warm embrace envelop him, and then a kiss on his cheek. He looked at his father and saw that he was crying.

"Da, what's wrong?"

"Nothing, son," his father responded. "I love you, Isaac. I love you more than anything. You're my beautiful boy."

They sat in a silent embrace as the holographic soccer players waited for another match to begin.

"Where's Liam, Da?"

"He's in my lab downstairs cleaning up for me. He's got some work to do down there, then he'll be up to play with you. I'm going to work from home today in the lab so we can spend more time together. I'm sorry I've been away so much, Isaac. I'll work from home more often, okay?"

"Okay, Da."

"Alright. I'm going to go down now, and I'll send Liam up."

"Can I go down in the lab and help you? Can I, Da?"

"No, Isaac. Remember our agreement. You mustn't. Not right now, okay?"

"Okay, Da."

His father hugged him, kissed him, and then left. Isaac reset the game to play again.

He played several more matches but grew more bored with each one.

"Where's Da, Carrie?" he asked his companion.

"He's in the home lab, Isaac."

"I want to go down. Da said Liam was coming to play soccer with me."

"I don't think you should go, Isaac. You know your father doesn't want you to go to the lab and disturb him while he's working. He should be back up soon for lunch."

Growing angry, Isaac thumped the controller down. He got up and walked to the lift pod. It sensed his presence and opened to carry him down.

~*~

Isaac waited as the lift brought him below ground to his father's lab. It came to an almost imperceptible stop, and the door opened. He peered down a dark corridor, unfamiliar with this new world within his own home.

"Da?"

He looked over his shoulder at the lift pod and considered going back, his fear of the unknown beginning to overtake him. He heard a sound farther down the hall.

"Da?"

He crept along, hugging the wall for security. He passed a storage room lined with rows of deactivated test androids, standing silently in formation, as if waiting for a command.

"Da?"

The hum of electronics increased as he progressed. He could see a pod entrance toward the end, and it encouraged him to continue. He tried to envision his father and Liam behind the door, rather than the horrible things his imagination was suggesting. He was afraid to go forward, yet scared to go back. Only the promise of his father beyond moved him forward.

"Da? Betsy? Liam?" He edged toward the door, the hum now louder, turning to a reverberating thrum. He could feel the vibration of it through the wall. The cool surface no longer felt comforting to him. He edged along nonetheless.

"Da?" He reached the pod entrance, and it opened silently on his arrival. The glow from inside hurt his eyes, blinding him for a moment. He stood there and waited until he could see, afraid to step forward into the unknown without his vision to guide him.

Standing just inside the entry, he turned to leave, but the portal had shut behind him. He turned around again and blinked, the scene now coming into focus.

Liam sat across the room facing him, motionless and expressionless. His father and Betsy sat at a large control board, with their backs to him.

"Liam," he said softly. His friend didn't answer. Isaac's mind clouded with fear, confusion, and concern, as it had that first time he had seen Liam hurt on the soccer field. He couldn't force what he saw to make sense.

The bright lights of the room shone on Betsy's cranial dome. They also reflected from Liam's. Isaac moved his gaze from his friend's head to his long hair, which lay on a table near him.

"Liam!" he finally shouted, as he began to run across the room.

His father and Betsy turned simultaneously at the sound.

"Oh, no!" Harley exclaimed, rising from his seat. Betsy was already in motion, and she stopped Isaac as he passed them.

Harley scooped Isaac up as he strained to get to Liam. "It's okay, son. It's okay."

The boy became hysterical, twisting in his father's arms, trying to see, still trying to make sense of things.

"Liam is dead? Da? Liam is dead? Liam's not talking. Liam!"

"No, no, son," his father kept saying, soothing Isaac by gently stroking his hair and rubbing his neck. "He's okay. Let me show you."

Isaac still struggled to understand. He decided to trust his father.

"I want to talk to Liam."

"Alright, just watch, Isaac." Harley led him to where Liam sat and replaced his hair. It snapped into place with a magnetic click.

Liam now appeared normal to Isaac, other than his stillness and silence. "I want to talk to Liam, Da. Wake him up."

"I will, Isaac. But first, you have to understand. Liam is like Betsy and Carrie. He's a companion. He's your companion friend...or brother. But it has to be our secret, okay? Nobody knows. Only you, Betsy, Carrie, and me."

Isaac struggled to make sense of what his father was saying. Harley went to the console and waved his hand over a section, and Liam's eyes opened. "Liam, disengage from the mesh," Harley commanded.

Liam rose from the chair as if he had just woken from a nap, and finally, everything looked normal again to Isaac.

"Hi, Isaac," Liam said.

Isaac ran to him and embraced him.

Harley allowed them a few moments of silent bonding before interrupting. "Liam, it's important to understand that Isaac knows that you are an android. This must be kept from all other humans. Is that understood?"

"Yes, sir," Liam answered.

"Isaac, do you understand that this must be a secret, only for us?"

Isaac still felt confused but was happy to have Liam back. "Yes, Da. Our secret."

"Good, because I'll have something very exciting for you soon. Something you have wanted more than anything. Now let's all go and have some lunch."

21 Connection Lost

HARLEY SETTLED into his comfortable home lab chair and took a deep breath. Betsy sat next to him, composed and attentive. Her cranial dome glowed as she meshed with the equipment.

"Begin test preparation," Harley commanded. He glanced around his cramped lab to ensure everything was ready. The simulated chimpanzee stared back at him from one screen. The test android sat silently, eyes closed, in a DroidMesh station enclosure nearby.

A shrouded enclosure on the far side of the room wiggled as the animal within moved about.

"Betsy, let's start by repeating the last test that Susan and I did together," Harley said.

"All parameters are configured, sir."

He glanced at the one personal item he allowed in the small lab—a picture of himself and Isaac, their heads tilted together, smiling. Looking at it quickly bolstered his determination. He was thankful for the lack of distractions in this environment, and the ability to focus only on the task at hand. *I'll do this for you, son.*

For a moment he felt terrible about categorizing Susan as a distraction. *She's a good woman. She doesn't deserve that...* He immediately pushed the thought away.

"Begin test sequence," he ordered.

The lab jumped to life. Waveforms danced, lights flashed, and diagnostic messages flowed across digital screens. Harley leaned forward, pivoting his head to take in as much of the information as he could.

"Connection successful," Betsy announced in a monotone voice.

"C'mon..." Harley whispered.

The simulated chimp stirred. The android opened his eyes and began to look around.

"Connection dropped," Betsy reported.

The android closed his eyes and, to Harley at least, the chimp appeared pleased. Harley leaned back in his chair.

"The result was as expected," Betsy said. "Don't be discouraged. As you know, Mr. Harris, it's important to replicate the last result as a way to confirm that all environmental conditions here are the same as the last test in the Robotics Complex lab. From here, we move forward."

Harley looked over at her and smiled. "You're right, Betsy. Let's do this."

They ran through parameter changes and repeated the test in lock-step. Harley took pride in remaining as calm and collected as his creation. At times he paused to admire her. *Disciplined, determined, beautiful.*

Hours passed without notice. Harley celebrated their small advances and tried to contain his frustration at the lack of more significant successes.

"Let's stop for a while and discuss this, Betsy. Tell me what you're thinking."

"After further analysis, there does seem to be a delta between this environment and the Robotics Complex lab. My calculations indicate that the delta is somehow contributing to our progress in this environment."

"Please report the delta condition that you feel is most likely to be a factor in the variable results, Betsy."

"The test is dependent on the almost imperceptible human brain waves connecting with the receptors in the android firmware."

"I know, I know," he said. "Get to the point, already."

"In the Robotics Complex lab, there is far more electronic equipment. In the home lab…"

"That's it!" He jumped out of his chair and leaned down to kiss Betsy, something he had never dared to do before. He lingered there for a moment, amazed at how the texture and warmth of her lips resembled that of Susan's. *I did an excellent job with the synthetic skin.*

The gynoid turned her head and looked at him blankly as he stood back up.

"Sorry, Betsy. Sorry. I got carried away. You got it, though! The lab is the problem!"

"Yes, that is my conclusion as well," she responded.

They went through the lab, turning off all unnecessary equipment. Harley rubbed his hands together as they both regained their seats.

"Alright. Begin test sequence," he instructed.

He observed as the initial test events transpired as they had before.

"Connection successful," Betsy reported.

The chimp stirred again. The android opened its eyes, and then looked down to spot a synthetic banana on the table next to it. The simulated chimp became less animated as it realized it could control the android with its thoughts. The android reached for the banana.

Suddenly, the test android began to twitch and then jerked spastically. Its arms and legs flailed where it sat in the DroidMesh station. The chimpanzee howled in frustration, and the android went limp.

"Connection lost," Betsy said.

"No kidding," Harley responded with exasperation.

He thought for a few moments. "Turn off the rest, Betsy." The lights, monitors, and consoles all dimmed and then turned dark.

"Turn off the electronic geofence enclosure around the DroidMesh station, Betsy. It's the closest and most likely source of interference."

"Sir, I want to remind you of the possible consequences…"

"Please follow my instruction, Betsy."

She did as he asked.

They sat in almost complete darkness, only the dim emergency lighting illuminating the android and the two scientists. The simulated primate was no longer visible on the darkened monitor.

"Begin test sequence," Harley ordered.

Everything that had happened before repeated itself. Harley clenched his hands as the test android reached for the banana again. This time it removed it from the table and held it up, scrutinizing it.

"Amazing. Incredible," Harley said beneath his breath. His heart pounded, and his palms were sweaty as he watched the android's primate-like motions.

"Alright! Good enough for today's testing, Betsy. I'm tired, and I want to go spend some time with Isaac. Please shut everything down and clean up. I'll see you upstairs in the living quarters after you're through. Let's review the logs from today and prepare for the demo to the Robotics Council. I'll deploy the BrainMesh protocol to the global planet network."

"Yes, sir. Congratulations. Don't you think we should replicate the test a few more times?"

"I'm satisfied and exhausted. Isaac needs me. We're done for today. I couldn't have done it without you, Betsy."

"Thank you, sir," she responded.

Harley thought he detected a slight, satisfied smile on her face.

22 Distractions

SUSAN CHECKED THE TIME and considered calling Harley to say she had grown tired and wanted to go to bed. She sat back on the lounge and called up a favorite comedy on the entertainment module.

She woke to an announcement that a skycar was approaching. She moved to her grooming station to check her appearance and then muted the movie just as Harley came through the entrance.

Harley rushed to embrace her. "Susan, you're not going to believe it. It's so amazing. Let me fill you in on everything that happened."

She offered a light hug in response.

"What's wrong?" he asked.

"Nothing, it's just late. I thought you'd be here a while ago."

He walked around the room excitedly as he began to describe the day's events.

"Sorry, sorry. It's just that we—I mean I—finally made some progress in the testing, and lost track of time."

She sat down and crossed her arms. "Testing?" she asked. "I thought you weren't going to the lab today. 'Take a break from it,' I think you said."

"Right, yeah, but we did some of the testing from my home lab—to see if there might be a difference in the results."

"Sampson was right," she said to herself.

"What?" he asked.

"Nothing. So…you did more testing? With Betsy?"

"Well yes, of course."

He finally seemed to be picking up on why she was angry. *Clueless*, she thought.

He rushed to her again, gathering her in his arms and kissing her gently. "I'm sorry. I just thought I'd try a few quick things. I didn't want to call you over there to work after you'd already made plans for the day." He looked into her eyes sheepishly.

She lay back down on the lounge, and he sat next to her. The movie continued in silence.

"Anyway," he continued, "after we calibrated everything at the home lab the same as the Robotics Council lab, we got the same results. So that was a good thing. Then we went from there, trying to figure things out. Betsy discovered that it was the electromagnetic interference from all the lab equipment! Can you believe it?"

"Yay, Betsy," Susan said flatly, watching the actors go through their paces.

Harley got up and began walking around the room animatedly. "So, that got us *almost* there. The android reached for the stimulus and then went haywire. Some kind of spastic event, probably due to the shaky connection."

"Betsy is a useless pile of circuitry," Susan said, testing her theory that he wasn't listening.

"Then I got all crazy; we were so close at that point. I got up, turned off all the lights and equipment, and bingo, the monkey made the android pick up the banana and inspect it."

She continued watching the muted movie, feeling his gaze on her as he waited for her reaction.

"Crazy, right?"

He came back to the lounge and sat next to her.

"Hey, you aren't mad, are you? This is good. It's good for us. We have the council demo coming up, and now we're ready for it. Exciting, right?"

She turned abruptly to face him. "Why don't you do the demo with Betsy? What do you need me for? Stay in your android world, Harley. I'm a distraction from your work. I'm not sterile like her."

The excitement drained from his face. "Oh. No, Susan. Of course not. I like your distraction."

"So I *am* a distraction."

"No," he stammered. "I mean…I need you…"

"Harley, I don't think you were honest with me. You put me in a bad position by not telling me about this. I suspected you were working on the project without me, both in the Robotics Council lab and your home lab. Sampson was asking lots of questions when I met with him."

He tried to lie next to her, and she pulled away. "I'm sorry. This is important to me, so I've been bearing down on it. I need to do this, for Isaac. He's suffering every day. I didn't want you to feel like you had to put in the same hours that I have been."

She remained silent and sorted through her conflicting emotions. She felt Harley was at some kind of crossroads and in conflict about her role, both in the project and his life. "You need to make decisions, Harley…"

He put his arm around her and kissed her. She resisted at first but then gave in. They broke their embrace and lay quietly for a while.

"You need to stay focused. Your love for your son is clouding your judgment on this project, and it's becoming obvious to Sampson and probably others. Sampson is asking questions."

"I understand. Of course, the project benefits society, but Isaac too. I just hate to see him suffer. I hate what others put him through. I hate to see him wanting the simple things others have and take for granted. He'll never have anyone but me, Susan."

She felt herself softening, becoming sad as she considered that Isaac might never find love. *Like me.* She leaned over and kissed Harley, lying against him. Cupping his face, she felt the wetness of tears on his cheeks.

"Sometimes I don't know if what our society has done is right," she said. "We've homogenized ourselves too much. Society needs people who are different. We could've kept that. We washed it away because we were too concerned about disease, forgetting that some parents, like you, might want and love kids that aren't perfect. We order our children as if from a menu.

"When I watch these old movies, sometimes I feel a nostalgia for the way things were back there, even though I was never part of it."

"It's funny," Harley said. "Back in that world, through various times in history, they actually tried to do the same type of cleansing. They called it eugenics, 'good genes,' but their efforts were mostly tainted by the flaws humans had back then. The German Nazis were trying to use it as a way to build a superior race, through breeding only those they considered pure, sterilizing and massacring everyone else. That's when it became a thing to fear."

"I read about that, but there was more success with eugenics later, wasn't there?" Susan asked.

"Yes, scientific research brought breakthroughs in genetic medicine, prenatal testing, and other areas. But that was before the Proving, when they were afraid they were tampering with the domain of a divine supernatural presence. That one belief, that fear, held them back from so much."

"I like to read the works of fiction from the Old World. It's so interesting, how they always viewed themselves as being on a path to a dystopian future, where it's really utopian here. If they had only known."

"Well," Harley said. "It was dystopian for the vast majority of them. The ones who didn't make it out. Such a small fraction made it...the ones who prepared...the ones who saw the path that the Old World was on."

"Let's talk about something less depressing," she said. "Like Sampson."

"Oh, funny," Harley said. "Not by much."

"That meeting he called me to wasn't much more than a fishing expedition. I think Sampson's actually worried that you'll be successful. He's always had a competitive thing with you. I think he's bent on stopping the project."

"I know," Harley responded. "I can't have it. It's another reason I moved to the home lab. I have to do this, for Isaac."

She unmuted the movie but turned the volume low. She nestled against him as they both put the conversation behind them and let the story take them away.

When she woke, he was gone.

23 Stop, I Command

THE ROBOTICS COUNCIL peered down in anticipation as Harley and Susan prepared their demo. Their worktable held an array of monitors, whose images were also displayed on the screens above. They showed the simulated chimpanzee and various diagnostic panels.

Next to their table was a transparent electronic enclosure, outlined in blue light, in which the test android sat as if sleeping. Betsy sat on the other side of him in observational mode, as Harley had instructed.

"You seem to be behind schedule, Harris. How much longer?" Sampson's voice echoed down from above.

"We're just about ready," Harley responded, quickening his pace.

"Don't let him rush you. We need to be sure everything is right," Susan whispered to him as they worked.

Finally, Harley stood and addressed the council.

"First I'd like to say that we're still at the beginning of our research. Per the council's guidelines, we're only using a simulated primate, not a real one. That introduces certain variables, as does giving this demo outside of the lab environment. Please take this into consideration as you view our demonstration."

"Get on with it," Sampson instructed.

"A bit of patience, please, Mr. Sampson," Sinclair, the council leader, admonished.

Harley tried to keep his composure. His nerves were on edge. He sat back down next to Susan. "Is everything ready?" he asked her.

"Ready," she responded with confidence.

He glanced up at the council, then back to the monitors.

"Begin test sequence," he instructed.

The monitors jumped to life. The ones above him were intimidatingly large in his peripheral vision. He tried to focus on the smaller displays directly in front of him, in an attempt to pretend he was in his comfortable lab environment.

Susan's presence next to him was comforting, but he longed for Betsy's clinical and focused assistance. He wished he hadn't agreed to reduce her role as a peace offering to Susan.

"Connection successful," Susan reported.

He smiled and was about to announce their status to the council when she interrupted.

"Connection dropped."

"It's okay, it's okay," he said to the group above, without looking at them. "We encountered this in the lab. It's purely environmental, is all. One moment please."

He muted their microphones. "Susan, turn off anything that's not necessary. Kill our monitors; we'll observe via the overheads."

She did as instructed, and they reinitiated the test sequence.

The connection sustained this time, lasting longer, but then dropped again. Harley felt his face grow hot.

"This clearly isn't ready," Sampson called from above. "I move to end to this waste of our time."

"Give it a few minutes, Mr. Sampson," another council member requested.

Harley began to feel a sense of panic. "Susan, kill the geofence barrier around the enclosure. I think it's what caused the problem last time. We removed it, and everything worked."

She looked at him with a shocked expression. "Harley, I don't advise that…"

"Just do it, please," he pleaded. "Please, Susan. It's how it worked before. Nothing adverse happened. It's just a simulation.

"Just one more moment," Harley called to those above him.

Harley looked at the small photo of himself and Isaac on his monitor and touched it with a finger.

Susan pushed a sensor to eliminate the barrier. The electric blue lights bordering it disappeared.

"Begin test sequence," he instructed.

"Connection successful," she said.

He waited for a few moments to ensure it wouldn't break. "The primate and android have established a BrainMesh connection," Harley informed the group. He watched, hands clenched into fists and palms sweating into his fingers. "C'mon," he whispered to himself.

The simulated primate on the monitor began to stir. The test android opened his eyes and looked around.

"The primate has realized that he is controlling the android, that he can see through its eyes, hear through its ears, and control its motor functions," Harley said.

The test android looked around and spotted the bunch of bananas that sat on the table next to it. The simulated primate became more animated as it made the discovery. The android picked up the bunch and removed a single banana.

"The primate has discovered the bananas through the android," Harley told the group. "The android has no prior programming to be able to do any of this by itself. It's running a dumbed-down shell version of the firmware. Its own intelligence is suspended, as it would be if a human meshed with it."

Harley continued. "Observe—the android peeled the banana as a primate would, from the tip rather than the stem."

They watched as the banana's casing was stripped. The android then took a bite of the banana, tried to chew, and then spat it out.

The council laughed. Harley, surprised by the action, hoped the levity would help their mood. "Hopefully, they'll allow us to use the live chimp now," he whispered to Susan.

His thoughts had sidetracked him. He didn't notice that the android had thrown the banana to the floor and stood up, looking enraged. The simulated chimpanzee became animated.

"I think we should quit while we're ahead," Susan said quickly.

"I believe the primate is becoming angry because he can't taste it. Androids don't have taste sensors, of course," Harley reported to the council while moving to shut down the test. "Shut it down, Susan, quickly," he whispered.

"Uh oh," Susan said, repeatedly pressing a sensor that was not responding.

"Everything will be fine," Harley said to the council in a loud but shaky voice as he furiously worked to end the demo. "Shut down test sequence," he commanded. He heard a gasp from above.

The android got up from the DroidMesh station and knuckle-walked around the lower area. Appearing confused, it rose up and walked toward the worktable, beating its chest angrily. It reached out and slapped a monitor to the floor, then approached Harley and Susan.

"Get out, Susan," Harley said, stepping between her and the android. The simulated chimpanzee on the monitor above raged and howled.

The test android grabbed Harley by his lab coat and lifted him off his feet. There was a cacophony of sound and panic from the observers above. Harley looked down at the android, terrified.

"Stop, I command," he instructed, then realized that the shell firmware was not equipped to understand or obey him. He was purely at the mercy of the simulated chimpanzee; both it and the android his own creations. An idea emerged from his panicked mind.

"Betsy, wake. Please help me," he pleaded.

He heard Susan scream as he saw motion from the corner of his eye. Betsy got up from her seat and grabbed the test android's head between her hands, giving it a violent twist. The electronics in the test android's exposed cranial dome sparkled and flashed brightly. Betsy continued twisting until the android's head was completely reversed. The two androids looked each other in the eyes for a moment, until Betsy yanked the head off and let it fall to the floor.

The test android went limp, and Harley fell to the floor in a heap. He looked over to Susan, who had fainted.

"Thank you, Betsy," he said.

"We've seen enough! This is an abomination!" Sampson screamed, standing above.

This time the other council members didn't rein him in. Harley looked up to see them all standing and looking down at him with disapproval.

24 Stars Above

THE STARS ABOVE seemed to call to Isaac as he lay in his bed looking up through the transparent dome. He wondered if there was a place up there with only people like him.

He dreamed of what it might be like to live like any other person: loving, working, playing. He decided if there were such a place, he would be kind to anyone there who might be different.

"Carrie approaching," the pod announced.

"Come in, Carrie," he said.

She entered and sat on the bed next to him.

"Are you okay, Isaac?" she asked. "It's early to be in bed. Your mood has seemed to be down lately. Do you want to talk to me?"

"I'm okay. I'm just sad sometimes. I don't see Da much. Nobody likes me."

"That's not true. I like you, and Liam likes you. He was looking for you. He wanted to play virtual soccer for a while before he went out."

"I'm talking about humans. Humans don't like me. You're not human, and Liam's not human. You're programmed to like me. I think Da played a trick on me with Liam and I'm mad about it."

"Liam and I are still your friends. When you're down, you have to rely on your friends and your family. Your father loves you. That's why he's been working so hard. He's working on something that will help you."

"I hope it's a skycar that will take me to one of those." He pointed to the stars above. "Maybe one has people like me. Friends and girls like me."

She looked up and then placed a hand on his knee. "The probability of that happening is low, Isaac. So the best course of action would be to make things work here. You're at an age that's difficult for any human. There are a lot of emotions at play."

They stayed together for a while, Isaac gazing up through the dome.

"I'll go and find your father and ask him to come speak to you," she said.

"I can't find him again. He's hiding in his secret place. He's not here, and he's not downstairs in his lab. He doesn't answer his communicator."

She rose and leaned down to put her hand on his face. "I'll find him. Try to cheer up, Isaac."

He watched her leave and again focused on the star field above. They twinkled as if trying to say something, and he struggled to understand what it might be. As he began to doze off, the pod announced that his father was approaching.

His father entered and lay down next to him, and they watched the stars together.

"Carrie says that you haven't been taking much interest in school, or even virtual soccer, lately," Harley said.

"I'm just taking a break, Da."

"Hey, let's go play some virtual soccer. I'll beat you this time, Pelé!" his father said in an upbeat tone.

"Can we play tomorrow, Da? I'm tired."

A shooting star flew across the sky above, and then another.

"Isaac," his father said. "Please tell me you'll hang in there and trust me. I'll help you. Things will get better, I promise. But until then, I need you to go to school and do the best you can. Can you do that for me?"

"I will, Da. I'll do my best. Where's Liam, Da?"

His father hesitated. "He's...he went out for a while. He'll be back soon. Do you want me to tell him to come and see you?"

"No, Da. I'm going to sleep."

"Alright then, son. I'm going to get some work done. I'll be downstairs in the lab if you need me." His father kissed him on the forehead and left the pod.

~*~

Isaac grew bored with the stars and sat in front of the communication console. "Call Kim, please," he asked the system.

The connection completed, surprising him. Kim appeared, sitting on the floor in her personal pod surrounded by art materials.

"Hi, Isaac!" she said.

He became excited that she seemed so happy to see him, and he wished he had gone to the grooming pod to clean up and try to fix his hair.

"Hi, Kim. What are you doing?" he asked.

"We're making some signs and banners for the big soccer game next week. It's the last game of the season. I hope you're going to go this time, we've missed you!"

She said 'we.' "Is Ralph there?" He became scared that his nemesis might be present and thought about disconnecting the session.

She didn't answer immediately, and he pulled back the view. As he did, he saw Liam sitting on her bed. His head was down as he worked on a banner, his long hair flowing over his face. He looked up and smiled.

"Hi, Isaac. I'll be home soon if you want to play virtual soccer."

Isaac felt tears beginning to well up in his eyes. "Liam can't love you, Kim. He can't ever love you," he said.

Kim looked at him with a confused expression. "Isaac...I..."

He disconnected the session and went back to his bed and the stars above.

25 My Sweet Jessica

HARLEY WATCHED from the home lab as his son's heart broke again. He turned off the remote camera feed and put his head in his hands.

After allowing himself a moment of pity for his son, he began to think. Anger, love, and determination spurred him on.

"Prepare the lab, Betsy," he commanded. "I'll be right back, and we'll begin where we left off. Analyze the data from the failed demo, and place a new test android into the DroidMesh station enclosure."

"Yes, sir," she responded, moving into action. "But I have already analyzed the data from the failed demo."

He stopped in his tracks and turned to face her.

"Did you reach a conclusion?" he asked.

"Yes. There was an unusually high level of radio and electromagnetic activity for that room. It spiked at the time we commenced the demo, and it stopped after the demo failed."

"Sampson!" he shouted.

"I feel there is a strong probability that Mr. Sampson interfered with the demo," she said.

"Get everything ready. I'll code a firewall algorithm to filter out any noise and parse only clean BrainMesh traffic. I'll be back shortly."

His anger propelled him as he left the lab and stormed through the home complex's below-ground corridor. He reached the end and stood before a blank wall.

"Reveal the hidden living pod," he instructed.

"I have identified your iris and voice, Mr. Harris. Please provide further information to allow authorized access."

"The passphrase is 'Jessica.' Open," he instructed.

An opening appeared, and he passed through it into a living pod that seemed just like any other part of the home complex.

Comfortable furniture filled the room. A large bed sat in the middle, the back raised so its occupant could watch a video from the entertainment system. A movie from the Old World played out quietly, its actors involved in a love scene.

On a table next to the bed was a beautiful bouquet of simulated Old World flowers and a picture of Isaac. The room smelled of lilacs, her favorite fragrance.

Several android attendants moved about the room. One sat next to the bed, holding the woman's hand, the only visible part of her.

Harley paused to collect himself and then moved ahead to take the empty chair. It was always there, designated for him in his frequent visits.

He looked at her, finding the same empty expression as always. Beneath her blanket, he could see the outline of the equipment that was keeping her alive, forcing her lungs to breathe, pushing nutrients into her body, eliminating her waste, stimulating her brain in the hope that it would jump back to life. *The beautiful life that was always inside her. The one I took away.*

"Jessica," he began, before becoming overwhelmed by memories of their life together that were running through his mind. He took a few moments to collect himself.

"What's her status?" he asked the attending android nurse, forcing himself into a more clinical frame of mind.

"Jessica remains functionally the same, with no brain activity. Her physical condition continues to deteriorate."

He looked at her frail outline and reached up to stroke the brittle remains of her red hair and her hollow face. A pink-purple scar formed a ragged arc above her ear. He filled out the picture in front of him in his mind, into the beautiful, loving, fun woman he had adored with every molecule of his being. *I never should have tried to implant the neural lace.*

"Has the team found anything yet? Any way, searching your databanks and using the algorithms, to bring her back? I've made progress with BrainMesh. I'm almost there. If her brain works, I could mesh her into an android body. Is there any chance…"

The android faced him. "There isn't enough brain activity to support such a thesis, Mr. Harris. I'm sorry."

He swallowed hard. "How long, then, in your estimation?" he asked.

"The human species is strong and unpredictable, even in a condition such as this. Jessica is a strong woman, in whatever presence she has remaining, which may only be her human spirit. We androids do not know enough about that to make a determination based on it."

"Estimate how long," he commanded.

"We estimate a short timeframe based on her current trajectory, sir. She has been in this state a long time, and it isn't possible to maintain it forever."

"Can we have some privacy?" he asked the androids in the room. They left the pod in unison.

He looked her over. "Jessica, honey. It's me. I hope you can hear me. I love you. I still love you. I can't function in this life without you, but I have to, for Isaac, for the promise we made to each other before the accident. Before…everything went wrong."

He took her other hand in his and began stroking the back of it with his thumb. *She always liked that.*

"Where I was with BrainMesh back then…it was so crude. I never should have allowed you to talk me into trying it. I know you wanted to help Isaac, but it was too early, honey. Much too early. Much too dangerous…"

He looked at her and squeezed her hand as grief overtook him again. He leaned forward to lay his head on her chest and let his tears soak into her sterile bedding.

"Oh, Jess, my Jess. I want you back, please come back. Isaac needs you. I need you. I'm so sorry…we never should have tried it back then. I never should have let you be first. We should have come clean and just told the council what I was doing and gotten volunteers from Seclusion."

He picked up the image of Isaac as a small boy from the side table and countered his own argument.

"We were both desperate. The council never would've given us approval back then. They would have known it was just for Isaac. They were so upset that we hid the truth about him until he was born."

She stared ahead at the movie, and he followed her gaze. A young family was at a park, which was filled with a kaleidoscope of brightly lit amusements. The father was using an ancient video camera to film the children as they passed by on a ride, again and again, waving, laughing, and smiling. The mother beamed, happy to see her children enjoying themselves. A baby lay sleeping in a carriage between them, despite the cacophony of sound.

"If only we could go back there, Jess. If only they hadn't ruined it all. Like us, they didn't know what they had, and should've left it alone."

He returned his gaze to her blank face and wasted body. He could still see the old Jessica, but it required more of his imagination each time he returned. He let his thoughts drift, and it gave him time to stand back from everything that had been happening in his life.

"I'm starting to think maybe that's it, Jess. Maybe I need to just stop trying to do this, trying to make Isaac whole in some way. Maybe I need to be thankful for who he is and teach him to be thankful too, even though he'll never have the things he wants so much in life."

He studied her, wanting some kind of reaction, some kind of sign. "I don't know what to do, Jess. Please tell me what to do. I know I promised to continue for him if anything bad happened to you, but I don't know if it's right anymore."

Her eyes closed as she drifted into sleep. Harley stood and kissed her on the forehead before leaving.

He left the room and looked back. "Conceal the living quarters," he said. He watched as the seams for the entrance portal disappeared.

26 A Better Man

SAMPSON LEANED BACK in his office chair and waited for his prey. It wasn't long before the announcement came.

"Mr. Harris is approaching."

"Allow access," Sampson said.

He watched Harris make his way toward the office and noticed right away that the man's usual timid gait and demeanor were gone. Harley strode in with an angry expression.

This should be fun. Maybe he knows.

Harris entered and spoke before Sampson could greet him.

"You did it, didn't you? You screwed up my damn demo."

Sampson tilted forward and casually leaned onto his desk. "Easy there, Harris. You know that word is on the forbidden list. I won't report you, but don't repeat it. Have a seat. We need to talk."

"You sabotaged my demo, Sampson…"

"Easy, now. Call me Ken, or Mr. Sampson, please. Have a seat."

Harris paced back and forth in front of Sampson's desk. "So you admit it?"

"I admit nothing. It doesn't matter. Your experiment should succeed no matter the environment. What if this crackpot technology you're working on came to fruition and failed? People could be hurt by your robots running amok like the one in the lab." He watched with pleasure as Harris became angrier.

"You know it was a prototype. A demo. Of course, those precautions would be put in place before any production release. It doesn't matter, though, because Betsy has solved the problem."

Sampson decided to remain quiet until the tantrum was ended. Harris continued to fume, looking out at the landscape through the office pod's window. Then he seemed to catch himself and calmed. He placed his hands on the workstation and looked Sampson in the eyes.

"I know what you're up to. You've always had it in for me, and I've always been the better man. You don't like me, or my son, or Liam. You know my son is a better person than yours, despite his disability. You know that Liam has stolen Ralph's thunder on the soccer field. And it's just killing you.

"But guess what. We'll prevail because we are better. You can't stop us."

Sampson yawned and glanced at his monitors before answering.

"Right. About that. It's why I called you here. You haven't been in the lab as much as I expected since your failure, Harley. Why is that?"

His question took the other man by surprise. He sat back down before answering. "I've been taking a break. Thinking things over. Spending time with Isaac."

"That's a good approach, after that disaster. The council has taken some time to think things over as well. They've made a decision, Mr. Harris. They feel it's too soon for this type of technology. They don't see enough benefit to society as a whole. I have already notified and reassigned Susan."

He enjoyed Harris' stunned look and again remained silent to let it soak in. Harris closed his eyes. Sampson noticed him gripping his chair's armrests so tightly that his knuckles had gone white.

"That's wrong," Harris finally said. "This technology can help people."

"People like your son, you mean? He's the only one who needs that type of help."

Harris still appeared to be reining in his anger. "Maybe there could be others like Isaac. Maybe parents wouldn't want to cancel children like him if they could lead more normal lives."

"As I said, Harris, not enough benefit to society at this time. The decision has been made."

Harris appeared to be his reviewing his options.

"Don't do anything rash, Harley. You can make an appeal, as you know, but those take considerable time."

Harris began to rise.

"Please, stay seated. There's more. The council is concerned about you, Harris. You have stress factors that are no longer normal in our society. We aren't equipped for stress the way they were in the Old World.

"They feel that you should stand down for some time, and they've ordered a complete physical and mental review before you can resume your duties at the lab. I'm sure you'll enjoy the chance to spend more time with your son."

Harris stood slowly, as if struggling against gravity, and turned to leave.

"And Harris, don't compare my son to either of those two. Ralph informed me that you sent Liam over to work with Kim on some nonsense for the upcoming game. Did you do that to upset my son? As retribution, because you feel he's not nice to Isaac?"

Harris turned in the doorway. "Is that what all this is about? Your son's feelings getting hurt?"

Sampson laughed. "Not at all. But I must forewarn you that Liam's eligibility for the big playoff game next week is being challenged. He hasn't been with the team a full season. You might want to prepare him for that possibility. Isaac as well. Goodbye, Harris."

Harris walked through the exit to the office pod, then suddenly turned and came back in. Sampson looked up, delighted to continue the discourse.

"One thing," Harris said. "Who told you?"

"Who told me what?"

"Who told you that we were experiencing problems with electronic interference? Was it Susan?"

"Goodbye, Harris. I have work to do."

Sampson turned to his monitor and pretended to work until he saw Harris leave from the corner of his eye.

27 All Systems Ready

THEY BEGAN without conversation, having repeated the process many times over the preceding days. Their hands worked swiftly, setting parameters, then checking and double-checking everything. They worked with intent and knowledge that time was of the essence. Finally, they paused and looked at one another for final verification.

"Is everything ready, Betsy?" Harley asked.

"All systems are ready," she responded.

"Okay. We'll repeat the simulated test one more time, just to be sure."

He checked the test android in the DroidMesh station enclosure. The simulated primate now appeared to regard him without malice.

"Begin test sequence," he instructed.

He and Betsy observed their monitors, occasionally glancing at the subjects. The simulated primate found and inspected the stimulus through the android. Its frustration at not being able to consume the banana appeared to be contained. Harley allowed the experiment to conclude.

"Terminate test."

Harley sat back in his chair with satisfaction and enjoyed the moment. Betsy finished logging the test results and resetting the equipment.

When she had finished, she turned to him as if waiting for further instructions.

"Betsy, prepare the live primate."

"I must inform you that this command is in violation of the council's established guidelines for this project, sir."

"Override. You have my permission," Harley informed her.

"As you advise, sir."

He breathed a sigh of relief that the rogue firmware patch he had installed in her had worked, allowing the override. He watched as Betsy entered the caged enclosure and kept the chimpanzee calm by soothing and comforting it. When she had its confidence, bribing it with the synthetic treats it liked, she inserted a small device into its ear canal.

The chimp reacted by pawing at it, and she stood back to let it do so, knowing it could not be dislodged. She then distracted and soothed it again before providing more rewards and exiting the enclosure. She stood back to watch the monkey enjoy its treats, then sat back down at her station.

"Begin collecting the primate's brain waves and loading their signatures into the android's translation module," Harley said.

He worked feverishly, writing the software updates to the test android's firmware while she carried out his instructions. He looked over to the chimp, which was now resting in its cage.

They went on for hours, taking few breaks. Harley only realized they had worked through the night when he found himself struggling to keep his eyes open. *Sampson's bound to wonder what I've been up to at some point.*

He admired Betsy's stamina, his prize creation functioning flawlessly and gracefully under pressure. He looked at Betsy and saw the things he had looked for in Jessica during his last visit to see her. He saw the details he had subconsciously designed into Betsy, features from the wife he had loved so deeply. *She's got it all, except that red hair.*

He meandered down memory lane, replaying their most precious moments together, from the time they met to Isaac's birth. *Our precious, beautiful, imperfect child.*

"Sir?" he heard Betsy say as she shook him awake.

He struggled to regain his faculties, shaking off the cobwebs of what he hoped was a short nap.

"I think we're ready," she said.

The monitor displayed a message that his code changes had passed testing and were installed on the test android. The chimpanzee dozed in its cage.

Harley stood, stretched, and then took a long drink of water. He looked at the image of himself and Isaac on his monitor. He thought about his son and fought off the urge to keep going.

"I've got to see Isaac off to school, Betsy. We'll run the next test as soon as I return."

"I'll be ready, sir," she said, smiling.

28 A Parent's Love

CARRIE SAT ON THE BED and placed her hand on Isaac's coverings.

"Isaac, you asked me to let you sleep a little longer. I've come back to remind you that we have little time remaining to get you to school without being late."

"I don't want to go," his muffled voice responded. "I'm sick."

"Humans are no longer susceptible to illness, Isaac."

"I broke my leg."

"I don't detect any sign of injury or pain. Your indicators are all normal."

He felt Carrie remove her hand and waited, hoping she would go away.

"I'll take it from here. Please leave us, Carrie," he heard his father say. *Da is here.*

He felt the bed move as she got up, and then again as his father sat. He burrowed his head farther beneath the pillow and tried to will himself back to sleep.

"Isaac, it's your father. I need to speak with you. Please sit up and talk to me."

He rolled over and stared up through the dome at the olive sky and puffs of condensation rushing by. He avoided looking at his father.

"I thought we had a deal, buddy? That you would go to school and do the best that you can?"

"I want to do independent lessons, Da. I like it better. I don't like going there anymore. I don't want to go today."

"Isaac, you need to socialize. We're a small civilization here. We just can't survive without other humans. We need that."

"You're human, Da. We have each other."

"It's not enough. You need to have friends. Humans need each other."

A long, dark-blue skycar appeared above the dome, moving slowly across the horizon. His father seemed to spot it immediately, and he jumped from the bed to observe it more closely.

"What's the matter, Da?"

"Nothing…it's just a council car. We don't see them in this area much."

His father sat back down next to him but seemed to be fixated on the vehicle.

"Like I was saying…I need you to go today. It's crucial now. Carrie will be with you. Please, son. Please do it for me. Your mother would be disappointed in you."

He watched his father's eyes follow the skycar until it was out of view. "What's wrong, Da? You're scared or something."

His father appeared startled and looked into his eyes. "Isaac, I need you to go. Please."

Isaac started to get upset. "Da, you keep saying that everything is going to get better. It's getting worse for me."

His father took his hand. "Listen to me. Nothing is stronger than a parent's love for their child. A father's love for his son. My love for you. I wouldn't lie to you. Everything will be okay, very soon. You must trust me. Can you trust me?"

The skycar appeared again, this time coming from the opposite direction, moving in a line across the sky. Harley got up again to watch it, then sat back down.

"I'm scared, Da."

"Isaac, it'll be okay. We're running out of time…I mean…you're running out of time to get to school before it starts. Please go today, and we'll talk more after school about independent study. Okay? Please?"

He thought he saw sadness in his father's eyes, and he began to feel bad. "Okay, Da. I'll go."

His father got up quickly. "Good. Good, son. That's great. Thank you. Carrie, can you return and help Isaac prepare for school please?"

As the gynoid re-entered the room, his father leaned down and kissed him, then hugged him for a long time. "I love you," his father said. "Everything will be okay. I have to leave now," he added, looking back again at the skycar.

"Please move quickly," his father said to Carrie.

29 Unfamiliar Craft

H ARLEY RETURNED, feeling alarmed about the circling council skycar above, but invigorated about the urgency it gave to his quest. *It's time.*

"We must work fast, Betsy," he said. "There is little time. Are you ready?"

They picked up their pace, working methodically and in sync. They repeated the exercise, this time with the live chimpanzee.

Harley's excitement overruled his exhaustion, powering him through, step by step. They encountered many of the same obstacles they had with the simulated primate, but this time with the knowledge of how to overcome them. Betsy frequently stopped to calm the chimp, but it seemed to become more used to the experience each time they went through it.

Complications arose with the one last variable—the receiver/transmitter earpiece. It pained Harley to think about his earliest attempts to use it as a neural lace cranial implant, and the disastrous consequences for Jessica. Each time he allowed the thought, he reminded himself how hard he had fought her in that decision, how she had begged him, how they had argued so passionately about it.

Success finally came a short time later. They deactivated the test android and removed the earpiece, which seemed to infuriate the primate.

"I guess that kind of power could be easy to get used to," Harley mused.

"Sir, I must inform you that my power reserves are growing quite low, and my fluids need to be recycled," Betsy said.

"Oh, my. Of course, Betsy. We're about done here. Please go upstairs to your DroidMesh station and rejuvenate. I'm going to work a little longer to prepare for the next step. I need to write the software for the human command module. Humans are going to need to be in control of all BrainMesh functions when they link with an android host."

"But the council has shut down the program. There will be no human volunteers from the Seclusion Zone to test on, sir."

"Yes, well…I'm appealing the decision. We need to be ready when I get approval to continue. You're excused, Betsy. Thank you."

He waited until she had left, then turned on an array of monitor banks that displayed the environment around the home complex. The same skycar he had noticed earlier was there, circling ominously. *They're probably trying to hack in and eavesdrop.*

Shaking off his fear and fatigue, he began his work. He wrote lines of software at a furious pace, stopping to deploy and test them in a simulator module. This time it was he who wore the embedded earpiece rather than the chimpanzee.

He ran through the commands each time, using his thoughts to engage with the simulator.

BrainMesh connect android TestSubject02.

BrainMesh assume control.

BrainMesh release control.

BrainMesh disconnect android TestSubject02.

He repeated the sequence over and over until the basic commands worked, not daring to take the experiment further. He then wrote the code for additional commands, without testing them. When the full non-discretionary command set was complete, he put his head down on the table to rest for a moment. *Hopefully, today will be your last hard day, son.*

The home complex alert system jolted Harley awake.

"Warning, unfamiliar craft docking in the landing pod…"

"Warning, unfamiliar craft docking in the landing pod…"

"Warning, unfamiliar craft docking in the landing pod…"

"Warning, unfamiliar craft docking in the landing pod…"

He scrambled to shut down the systems and clean up the home lab while watching the council skycar on the overhead security monitors. It glided into the landing pod and came to a rest inside.

As he was finishing, he saw Sampson and several android Security Team members disembark. He left the lab in a rush and stood outside it.

"Conceal home lab two," he commanded. The entrance disappeared into the wall. He walked farther down the hall, until he came to the test android storage room.

"Conceal test android room." He continued down the hall and stopped before a blank space in the wall.

"Reveal diversion lab."

An entrance appeared. "Open," Harley instructed. An entrance portal appeared, and he walked through it, sitting down quickly and switching on the equipment at the workstation.

The alternate lab was a scaled-down facsimile of his main home lab. Harley hoped that his occasional use of it to build mundane firmware updates would be enough to mislead the investigators he knew were closing in.

He dashed around the table to an older-model test android seated in a DroidMesh station. Panic surged through him as he tried to run through the scenarios and outcomes of what might be about to happen. *I hope I can survive this. I hope Isaac can survive it. I'm so close.*

He had just sat back down and begun the pretense of writing code when another announcement came.

"Visitors approaching."

"Allow access," he said.

He was peering into the monitor with his fingers dancing across the table's sensors when they entered.

"That's enough, Harris," Sampson shouted as he entered the lab.

Harley jumped to his feet. "What is this? What're you doing here? This is my home."

Sampson stepped into the lab and looked around. "Just as I thought. Mr. Harris, you're in violation of the council's order to shut down BrainMesh. You've been continuing the project in this home lab."

"I'm doing research, Sampson. It's not the same thing. Different code bases."

Sampson looked at the Security Team. "Detain him."

He smiled at Harley. "You can tell it to the council at your hearing. For now, you'll be held in the Detention Area."

The android Security team approached and asked him to comply without resistance.

Harley turned to Sampson. "What about my son? He's all I have. He needs me here."

"He seems to do quite well without you," Sampson said with indifference. "He's a young man—it's about time he learned to function without his daddy doing everything for him. Besides, he's got his...nursemaid, the gynoid that's always glued to him."

"Shut down lab," Harley instructed. The monitors, test android, and DroidMesh station went dark.

"Take him to the skycar," Sampson ordered. "I'll be up shortly—as soon as I get done dismantling this lab and getting this stuff ready to be sent back to the Robotics Complex for analysis."

"You won't win, Sampson," Harley said. "It's you who belongs in Seclusion. You're the one who slipped through the cracks and doesn't belong in this society. You'll never be as good as my son or me. You'll see."

They reached the upper floor and walked past a dormant Betsy in her DroidMesh station.

"I need a minute," Harley said. The team conferred and agreed.

"Betsy, wake," he instructed.

She opened her eyes and took in the scene. "Is everything alright, sir?" she asked.

"Mr. Sampson is causing trouble for me. He's downstairs; don't interfere with him. I have to go with these androids, but I expect to be back soon. I'm sure they'll let me communicate with Isaac, but please stay here and maintain the home complex while I'm gone. Coordinate with Carrie and help her care for Isaac."

"Yes, sir. I will."

The Security Team escorted him toward the skycar station.

38 Assume Control

HARLEY PACED in his Detention pod. The limited accommodations frustrated him. He felt neutered without Betsy, and the realization hit him that in short order he had lost his job and access to both his work and his home.

As he thought hard to formulate a plan, the afternoon turned into evening. He watched the staff pass by his windows as they went about their daily schedule, ensuring that the detainees were well fed and comfortable. He lay down on the lounge and put on a movie, the same one he had been watching with Jessica during his recent visit.

He decided to catch up on his sleep. *I'm going to need to be rested and at my best.* He allowed himself to drift away while looking up through the dome of the facility into the sky full of stars overhead.

The glow of the rising twin suns filled the room and brought him slowly back to consciousness. He sat up and reassessed his situation, working through other outcomes and their probabilities of success.

He cleaned himself up and issued a command.

"Call Isaac."

His son's image appeared before him, seated at the workstation in his living pod.

"Where are you, Da?" he said immediately. "I'm scared."

"I'm okay, son. Something happened with work. I'll be back soon. Everything is alright."

"I'm gonna go to school today, Da. I'm gonna go because I love you."

Harley felt a warm surge of love for the boy flow through him. "That makes me happy, Isaac. You make me happy no matter what you do, son. I love you so much."

"I love you too, Da."

"I'll talk to you after school. Just remember, it's important to do everything Carrie and Betsy ask you to do. Exactly as they tell you, okay?"

"I will. Bye, Da."

The image faded as an attendant android approached and requested access.

"Enter," he responded.

"Mr. Harris, your hearing with the council has been scheduled for tomorrow afternoon."

"Please request a reschedule for the morning. I would like to attend Liam's soccer game in the afternoon," Harley asked.

"I will make the request, sir."

"Thank you. I also ask that I not be disturbed for the rest of the day. Please hold any messages, and I'll retrieve them later."

He watched as his own creation left. *Sometimes I think we'd be better off if they ran things, rather than humans.*

As soon as he was alone again, he blacked out the room and returned to his bed.

"Call Betsy," he instructed his communicator.

Her image appeared in the room. "Yes, Mr. Harris?"

"Betsy, I'd like you to go to your DroidMesh station and rejuvenate. Please make sure you also upload the new firmware that I scheduled for you."

"I'll go now, sir," she said as her image disappeared.

He lay prone and steadied his breathing, trying to completely relax. He reached up and placed a finger into his ear, to ensure that the earpiece was in place.

After he'd allowed enough time to pass to be sure she was in position, he closed his eyes. *Please let this work.*

Taking what he imagined could well be his last breaths, he summoned his courage, and it failed him. *I love you, Isaac.* He focused and tried again.

Emptying his mind completely, he issued the mental command as if he were speaking it to one of his androids.

BrainMesh connect android Betsy.

He felt a tingling throughout his brain as if receiving a mild electrical shock. A bloom of tiny sparks blossomed through every region of his mind, and then a continual low-energy pulse. A dull numbness. He was afraid to think, afraid to open his eyes. He breathed again, to verify that he was still alive.

Maintain the status quo—steady state. Adjust. Don't panic. Don't overthink it. Don't accidentally think a command.

He became accustomed to the new sensations and again summoned the courage to issue the next command.

BrainMesh assume control.

A surge flowed through him, this time emanating from his brain, branching out to what felt like every nerve ending in his body.

He opened his eyes, but they weren't his eyes.

The home complex room containing Betsy's DroidMesh station came into focus. His mind seemed confused at first but quickly adjusted. He now had two pairs of eyes, and he kept his own shut, fearing he would overwhelm and possibly short-circuit his brain. He still wasn't sure which aspects of the failed experiment had led to his wife's catatonic state. *Worst case, I join her, wherever she is.*

Realizing what was happening, he took a moment to let the experience wash over him. *Amazing.* He began the process of learning to operate his new extremities. First, the fingers, bending each one in turn. Then balling his hands up, flexing his wrists; then the elbows, finally extending each arm out in front of himself. He worked his toes, ankles, knees. He looked down and for the first time realized he was now in a woman's form.

Refusing to become distracted, he disengaged himself from the DroidMesh station and stood, wobbling at first. Training his mind each step of the way, he began his first steps. He felt the gynoid body lurch and stagger at first, and had to reach out for the wall to steady himself.

"Are you functioning properly, Betsy?"

He heard the question in his mind, not through his human ears. He recognized Carrie's voice.

He turned to face her and attempted to speak for the first time. "Yes," he started to say but realized he was using his own human mouth. He concentrated and tried again, trying to signal to his brain to use the other one available, as he would if deciding to use his left or right hand for a task.

"Yes, Carrie. I'm adjusting to a new firmware download from Mr. Harris. It seems to involve my internal gyroscope and requires some adaptation."

Carrie looked at him as if analyzing. He decided to try to distract her, wondering if he should have told her what he was going to attempt.

"Mr. Harris has given me some things to do in the lab. Please let me know when Isaac returns home, I need to speak to him."

"Yes, Betsy. I'll do so."

He left the room and made his way downstairs to the lab corridor, first entering the decoy lab. As he expected, he found it gutted. Sampson had had his team remove everything.

He went back into the corridor. "Reveal home lab one." The entrance appeared, and he opened it to step inside. Looking around, he was happy to find it untouched. He sat at his workstation, then jumped back, startled to see Betsy staring back at him from the reflection in a monitor.

He pulled his chair closer and examined himself in her image, running his hand over the smooth surface of his cranial dome, touching his face. Harley felt the contour of his female torso, unaccustomed to the new waistline he found — its curves and thin waist.

I can't be distracted. I've come this far; I can't let him down.

He initialized the equipment for the next step of his plan, then ran a few simple diagnostics and recorded notes in his log. He found himself wanting Betsy's help. His thought wandered to Susan, and he realized how much he missed her. He wondered where she was and if she was thinking about him. Then he remembered his wife.

Jessica... He decided to go to her again, cautioning himself to take care as he suddenly remembered he was in Betsy's form.

31 She's Gone

THE OTHER ANDROIDS TURNED as Harley entered the room as Betsy.

"Mr. Harris has asked me to check in on his wife," he said.

They didn't speak. Harley noticed immediately that something was off. *Something's wrong.*

He moved toward the bed, its back still raised, noticing for the first time that the usual life support equipment was not nearby. There was no movie playing. *I told them to always keep her favorite movies playing.*

He reached the bed just as the realization dawned on him. He looked at the other androids in shock.

"Jessica has passed. We've been trying to reach Mr. Harris," one of them said.

"No," he shouted, putting his hands on the sides of his head. "No, no, no!"

Feeling the smooth cranial dome brought him back. The androids were looking at him with perplexed expressions. He knew they were trying to make sense out of behavior that did not seem possible from one of their own.

He collected himself as quickly as he could. The sight of the empty bed threatened to overcome him again.

"When?" he asked.

"Thirty-seven minutes ago," one informed him.

He was struggling to decide whether to go to her body when Carrie summoned him on the communicator. He answered in audio-only mode.

"Isaac has returned from school," she said.

Jess has been gone for a long time. I just couldn't let go. She's at peace now, but I have to see this through for her. For Isaac. Harley made the difficult choice between the living and the departed and instructed the androids to follow the protocol he had laid out for this so long ago. "Please initiate the procedure for Jessica's remains. Mr. Harris has authorized me to issue this command."

He left the hidden room and made his way upstairs, stopping first to collect himself and push away his grief until he had time to deal with it.

When he continued, he encountered Liam first and whispered instructions in his ear before heading to Isaac's pod.

~*~

Isaac turned when he heard him enter. "Hi, Betsy. When is Da coming back?" he asked.

The question momentarily took Harley off guard as he continued to adjust. He wanted to run to his son and hug him but knew it would confuse and frighten the boy. *Stay calm…*

"He'll be back soon, Isaac. Hopefully tomorrow."

"I hope so. It's the big game. I want to watch Liam play," he answered with a hopeful expression. "I want Da to go with me."

"I'm sure he will, Isaac. Finish your assignments. You can be sure he'll ask you if they're done."

His expression turned glum. "I know," he responded. "I will, Betsy."

Harley moved into an empty pod to collect himself again. He sat as the weight of the most significant decision of his life bore down on him, along with the reminder of what had happened the last time he had made a similar choice.

Time is short. It's now or never. It's working fine. I'm doing okay. He'll be able to deal with this. I'll guide him through it.

He continued to talk himself into moving ahead with his plan until he was confident. His son's sadness and the possibility of what this procedure would mean for him pushed the scale toward moving forward.

Isaac was lying in bed when Harley re-entered his son's pod.

"Isaac, your father asked me to show you something in the lab. Come with me, please."

He rose slowly, as if reluctant. "Is Da in the lab, Betsy?" he asked.

"No, but he has something special for you there."

The hopeful look appeared again as Isaac began to follow him.

~*~

They arrived in the lab, where Liam sat in the DroidMesh station, this time with his hair intact.

"What's going on, Betsy? Why are we here without Da? What's Liam doing over there?" Isaac asked.

"Come over here, Isaac, and I'll explain." Harley guided him to the break area, and they sat on a lounge. Isaac looked around, appearing to grow nervous. The urgency of the situation helped spur Harley into the conversation.

"Isaac, your father said he would help you to enjoy the things that you want so badly. To play soccer, for example. Isn't that right?"

Isaac brightened. "Yeah, Da said so. He keeps saying it, though."

"Are you looking forward to that, Isaac?"

"Yeah," he responded after hesitating, still looking around the lab.

"Would you like that to happen today?"

"Yeah, Betsy. Where's Da?"

"Your father should be here tomorrow. He asked me to talk to you about this. Would you like to try an experiment, Isaac?"

The word seemed to scare him. *Lousy choice*, Harley thought. "Isaac, you know that Liam is an android, right?"

"Yeah. Liam is an android." He looked over to where his friend sat motionlessly.

"What would you think about becoming Liam for a little while, whenever you want to? Wouldn't that be fun? To play soccer and go to school as Liam?"

"I would like to be Liam. I can't be Liam, though."

"You can, for just a little while. Kind of like how you become Pelé when you play virtual soccer. Would you like to try it?"

Isaac seemed to understand. "I...guess so, Betsy. Are you sure Da said it's okay? We shouldn't be in here without him."

"Yes, very sure."

Isaac looked up at him and smiled.

32 I'm Normal

HARLEY, STILL IN THE GUISE OF BETSY, spent a long time in the lab with Isaac, going over the process and the instructions to connect and assume control. He made a game out of it, having his son relax in the lounge, clear his mind, and think the proper commands. He ran him through different scenarios many times, coaching him in the two simplified commands he would need to know.

"What thought would you put into your mind if you wanted to become Liam?"

"I would think in my head 'BrainMesh become Liam,'" Isaac answered.

"What thought would you put into your mind if you wanted to become Isaac again?"

"I would think in my head 'BrainMesh become Isaac,'" he answered.

They repeated the commands again and again until Harley was comfortable.

Finally, after they were both becoming weary of the drill, he decided it was time.

"I'm going to put something in your ear, Isaac. It will allow you to become Liam, for real."

The boy looked frightened again as Harley produced the insert. "It's okay. It won't hurt, I promise. Let me try. You want to be Liam for a while, don't you?"

"Okay, Betsy. I want to be Liam." Isaac leaned forward cautiously and permitted it to be inserted. Afterward, he immediately reached for his ear.

Harley gently intercepted his hand. "No, Isaac. You mustn't touch it. You'll get used to it being there."

When Isaac was lying prone and relaxed, he decided to try for the first time.

"Are you ready, Isaac?"

"Yeah, I think so," the boy said with his eyes closed.

"Alright then. Go ahead, relax and think the command. Stay calm. I'll be right here with you. Your father will be proud of you for being so brave."

Harley looked up at the video on the room's monitor and saw Betsy sitting next to his son. He waited as the tense seconds passed, looking from his son to Liam.

Isaac bolted upright, screaming. Harley comforted him.

"Remember, Isaac. Remember I said it would tingle and feel kind of nice? And then you would be Liam?"

"Yeah. It scared me, Betsy. It's scary."

"Let's try again. Now you know what it'll be like."

Harley held his hand, and they repeated the process.

Isaac appeared to be sleeping. Harley looked over to Liam just in time to see the android boy open his eyes and begin to look around.

Harley continued to observe without interrupting as Isaac became accustomed to the new experience and body. Harley saw wonder in the android's eyes, despite knowing it was incapable of that emotion on its own.

Harley held his breath as Liam slowly rose. He looked back to check on Isaac, and for the first time in a long time, he saw a smile on the boy's face.

Isaac, in Liam's form, took slow, measured steps away from the DroidMesh station.

Harley stood in incredulity at seeing his son for the first time in the body of an ordinary, healthy young man. He could *sense* it was Isaac, with a father's intuition about his own child.

Isaac now strode confidently across the room, and then ran to meet him in an embrace.

"This is fantastic, Betsy! I'm…normal!"

Harley held his son's surrogate android, looking over his shoulder at Isaac lying on the lounge.

At that moment, something felt profoundly wrong to him. Still holding back his grief for Jessica, his emotions slid from elation to deep sadness, and he considered calling the experiment off.

Isaac broke away from the embrace, smiling broadly. He leaped high into the air and landed gracefully.

"It feels good, Betsy. I feel strong. Wait until Da sees me!"

The words had come from Isaac, not the android. Harley moved over to him and retook his hand. "Try to think of the words coming from Liam, not yourself, Isaac. That's the way to speak through Liam."

Isaac moved to a shiny metallic server cabinet and looked at himself, running his hands through his hair.

"I'm normal, Betsy! I'm strong, and I'm not clumsy anymore. I can talk without my tongue getting in the way. I can think and speak clearly. Let's show Dad!"

Harley realized his son was no longer speaking in his usual slow, thick, slurred manner. He knew at that point that there would be no turning back. His thoughts turned to panic about how to manage the situation he had created. But underneath all his emotions, he felt the same sense of elation that he knew his son was feeling.

"Good. You did quite well. Let's practice becoming Isaac again."

Isaac looked at him with revulsion on his face. "Oh, no, Betsy. I don't ever want to go back to being Isaac again. Now I can play in the game tomorrow!"

Harley didn't want to send him back either. He had never seen his son this happy. He realized he had been away from his own body too long, and began to fear that someone would enter his pod in the Detention area and cause him to drop the connection.

"Isaac, I promised your father we would only do one short test. It's time to finish your assignments and get to bed for the night, so it won't matter if you're Liam or Isaac. We need to test your ability to become Isaac again. Let's do that, and then we can talk about you going to school as Liam tomorrow."

The last of what he said registered with his son. The idea apparently excited Isaac. Harley took advantage of that to get him to sit back down in the DroidMesh station. He walked back over to the break area to hold Isaac's hand and coached him to issue the command to switch.

He exhaled when Isaac opened his eyes and sat up, smiling.

"I was Liam! I can't wait to tell Da, Betsy!" he said.

Harley hugged him. "Hopefully, your father will be home tomorrow, Isaac, and you can do that. Now go on ahead upstairs and work with Carrie on your assignments." He made sure to remove the earpiece as he spoke, while Isaac was distracted.

He watched as Isaac left, and remained in the lounge to assess what had just happened. His exhilaration at the success of the test mixed with abject fear about the possible consequences of going down this path. The ethics of what he was doing pestered him. The nagging emotions were washed away almost immediately by the memory of his son's happiness and the smile on his face.

Harley logged his results and made a few adjustments to the code based on his observations. He then went upstairs to sit in Betsy's DroidMesh station and issued the commands to return to his human form.

He opened his eyes in the Detention pod and checked the time. *Early evening.* He summoned an attendant and was happy to learn that his hearing had been rescheduled to the morning, per his request. *Figures; Sampson can't wait for this.*

He realized he was exhausted, and allowed sleep to take him.

Android steps woke Harley. His long experience with them had given him a sixth sense. He looked around and realized it was morning.

"The council will see you shortly, Mr. Harris," the attendant informed him. "We have a skycar ready to transport you.

33 Bring a Witness

KEN SAMPSON WAITED, drumming his fingers on the table as he looked at the other Robotics Council members, trying to gauge their demeanor. He resisted the urge to break protocol and lobby his case against Harris.

Finally, Harris entered, accompanied by an android attendant from the Detention Zone. Sampson noticed that he was smiling and looking directly at him.

"Let's bring this to order," Sinclair, the council leader said. "Today's schedule is full, particularly since we squeezed this hearing in on late notice. Mr. Sampson, you have brought this allegation; please make your statement."

Sampson stood. "Mr. Harris has pushed this insane BrainMesh project for a long time, despite concerns from the council. I believe his only motivation is for the benefit of his son. I say that one mistake should not beget another."

He looked down at Harris, who seemed to refuse to take the bait and become angry. "Please don't refer to my son as a mistake, Mr. Sampson," he said calmly.

"Order," Sinclair commanded. "Your remark was out of line, Mr. Sampson, and seems to reveal a strong bias on *your* part. Please continue, with integrity this time."

Sampson thought he detected a slight grin on Harley's face. "We allowed Mr. Harris some leeway to do limited experimentation. His presentation to us was disastrous and exposed the extreme danger of this type of technology. We made a practical decision to discontinue BrainMesh. Mr. Harris violated the council's order by continuing the BrainMesh work in his home laboratory. I move that we send Mr. Harris to the Seclusion Zone for one year and that he be prevented from doing any further robotics work."

"And what evidence do you have?" the council leader asked.

"I can start with a witness," Sampson responded. "Please bring her," he asked a nearby attendant.

While he waited, Sampson looked down to enjoy Harley's concerned and confused expression. He waited until shock appeared on the man's face, and knew that Susan had taken her seat. He turned to her.

"Can you tell us what you know of Mr. Harris' activities in his home lab?" he asked her.

"I never worked with him there," she answered.

"I didn't ask that, Ms. Clarkson. What do you know of his activities there?"

"To my knowledge, he used it for mundane work, such as firmware updates to implement bug fixes and feature requests..."

"His activities, particularly regarding BrainMesh, in the home lab," Sampson corrected her, becoming angry.

"Harley...Mr. Harris...consumed himself with BrainMesh at the lab here in the Robotics Complex. He often worked late. I believe that's why he had to catch up on his regular duties after he went home, in his home lab."

Sampson caught a smile shared between the Harris and Clarkson and lost control.

"They're partnered! She's not reliable or objective. They've partnered, and she's lying for him!"

"Order!" Sinclair demanded again. "Ms. Clarkson, you may leave. Mr. Sampson, you're coming off like a raving lunatic. Do you have any further proof of your allegation?"

Sampson collected himself. "I do. We confiscated the equipment from his home lab, including one of his test creatures." He motioned to the man next to him. "One of our engineers here examined it. I'm sure it was all being used for BrainMesh. Harris was using it when we arrived at his home."

Harley stood again. "I'd like to ask your tech a few questions," he asked.

"He didn't come here to be cross-examined," Sampson interjected. "I didn't prepare for that."

"Go ahead, Mr. Harris," Sinclair said.

"I assume you examined the logs, analytic data, and diagnostic dumps from the equipment."

"Yes, Mr. Harris. I did," the tech responded.

Sampson thought his tone sounded reverent. *Not another Harris worshipper, I hope.*

"Did you find any indication of work being done that would be for a project like BrainMesh?" Harris asked.

"No, sir. Just the type of work that Ms. Clarkson described." The tech glanced at Sampson, who was scowling at him.

"I'd like to bring in a witness," Harley said.

"Who is that?" Sinclair asked.

"My companion assistant, Betsy. She was present for everything I did. She's out in the lobby."

"A robot shouldn't be testifying in a council hearing!" Sampson shouted.

"This *is* the Robotics Council, after all, Sampson. Androids can't lie. Bring her in," Sinclair asked the attendant.

Betsy came in and took a seat.

"Betsy, please display the data for the council," Harley asked her.

"This is ridiculous," Sampson said. "How can we trust what she saw? A robot can't be compelled to testify against its owner."

Betsy stood and projected a virtual image into the room. It was the same room, from back when they had done the demo for the council.

"I will overlay the demonstration replay with the output of a tool used to measure signal interference in different areas of the room," she said.

"This is absurd. A waste of time." Sampson said.

The scene reached the point where the demo had gone awry. The pattern of interference intensified in two areas: where Sampson sat, and around the test android.

"What is this? This has nothing to do with why we're here today," Sampson barked. "The robot has falsified this playback. I did nothing..."

He noticed the other council members looking at him skeptically.

"Mr. Sampson," Sinclair said sternly. "I've heard and seen enough of your bias toward Mr. Harris. Remain here while the rest of the council convenes in the conference pod to make our decision."

Sampson sat, red-faced and stunned, watching the members as they filed out. He looked at Harris, who was still smiling at him alongside his companion, who seemed to wear a satisfied expression. He decided to ignore them while he waited.

After an unbearably long break, the council filed back in.

"Mr. Harris," Mr. Sinclair began, "we apologize for the interference in your demo by one of our members. Despite that, the fact that things could go so wrong with this technology gives us great concern. The BrainMesh project will remain on hold until we can further assess society's readiness. As for the charge that you continued your experiments from your home lab, we see no evidence. You may be released from the Detention facility."

"Ridiculous," Sampson said.

"As for you, Mr. Sampson," the council leader continued, "your behavior has been unacceptable. You will spend one night in Detention as a warning and as punishment for interfering with the demonstration. You are fortunate no one was injured as a result of your reckless actions."

"You can't do that!" Sampson said, standing. "I'm going to my son's game this afternoon. I have work to do!"

The android attendants already had him by the arm, and the council began to file out.

34 Dream Come True

ISAAC WOKE FAR EARLIER than usual and scrambled from his bed. The suns had not yet risen, and neither Carrie or Betsy had detached from their DroidMesh stations to begin their morning routines.

He entered the grooming station and looked in the mirror, expecting to see Liam, and was disappointed when he didn't. He started to prepare himself for school before he realized that it wasn't necessary. He rushed to Liam's personal pod to pick out a uniform for school that day.

He was momentarily concerned that Liam wasn't in his bed, before remembering that he had been spending his nights in the lab, rejuvenating in his DroidMesh station, since his secret had been revealed.

Isaac spent time in front of Liam's grooming mirror with his eyes closed, going over how he would act and talk like Liam, as he'd been instructed. *It's important that I really be Liam, not Isaac. Nobody can find out, or I can't be Liam anymore.*

He thought about the day ahead and every dream he ever had come true. He played out scenes in his mind of talking to Kim at school without hearing pity for him in her voice. He ran through scenes of himself playing in the big game. He wished his father could be there.

Checking for daylight outside, he prepared his breakfast and made sure his assignments were done and filed. When he was through, he went back to Liam's pod.

He sat on the bed and imagined everything in there as his own. He was starting to feel sorry about having those thoughts when Liam entered the room.

"Good morning, Isaac," he said.

Isaac put his head down, embarrassed. "Good morning." He felt himself flush with guilt, feeling he was taking his friend's life from him, and couldn't come up with words to say.

Liam sat next to him on the bed. "So, are you ready?"

"What do you mean?" Isaac answered.

"To be me. Aren't you excited?"

Isaac looked down again. "I feel bad. If I'm you, then you won't be my friend. You're my only friend."

"You can be you whenever you want, and then I'll be there as your friend. You can be me whenever you want. Friends share things. Think of it as me sharing myself with you."

Isaac smiled. "That makes it sound better."

"Your father created me to help you. That's what I've been waiting for. I'm programmed for this, and if I could experience happiness, this is what would make me happy."

"But you can't play in the game if I play in the game as you."

"I'll be right there with you. It will be like we're both playing, won't that be fun?"

"I'm not good like you. I'm scared I'll mess it up. I'm nervous now, Liam. I'm not sure I can do it."

"We can do it. You'll have my legs, and I'll be with you. Guess what—your father made sure that I wasn't as smart about soccer as you. You know the strategy far better than I do. Imagine what a great team we're going to make!"

"Yeah," Isaac said. He was back to dreaming about the game, happy that he'd be sharing it with Liam, rather than leaving him out.

"Besides," Liam said. "It's just a silly game. Let's have fun. Who cares what happens?"

"What about Kim?" Isaac asked.

"Just be yourself. You're better at talking to her than I am. You have emotions; I don't. It's real for you. I can only fake it based on what's programmed into me. It's the same logic: have fun, and who cares what happens?"

Isaac noticed for the first time that the suns had risen and it was finally light outside.

Carrie and Betsy entered together.

"Where's Da, Betsy?" Isaac asked. "You said he'd be here today."

"He's working on it. He wants to come home to see you. He said good luck, and that he loves you. So, are you two ready?" she asked.

The agreed in unison and got up from the bed, following the two gynoids downstairs to Harley's lab.

A short time later, only the three androids returned.

Isaac, in the guise of Liam, walked confidently in front of the gynoids.

Carrie gave him last-minute instructions. "You father asked that I notify the school that you'll be studying independently, Isaac. That's where they think you'll be. I can't go with you, as I'll be home waiting for you to become Isaac again when you're ready."

"I don't need anyone to go with me, Carrie. Betsy can take me in a skycar."

35 Do Your Best

ISAAC ENTERED THE SCHOOL early and as if in a dream. He felt overcome by a mix of nervousness and excitement and ducked into a rest pod to steady himself before going to class. He was happy to find the pod empty and stepped in front of a reflector panel to check his hair.

Standing there looking at Liam still confused him. He straightened his uniform, touched his face, and ran his fingers through his long hair, feeling the hard cranial dome beneath it. He turned from side to side, examining himself from all angles.

When he faced front again, he saw Ralph behind him. A shock of fear coursed through him, and he suddenly wished he were home safe, as Isaac.

"Having fun admiring yourself, pretty boy?" Ralph sneered.

Isaac turned, unsure what Liam would say.

Ralph shoved him backward. "Are you staying away from Kim, like I asked you?"

"Yes," Isaac said softly.

Ralph stepped directly in front of him, so close they were nose to nose. "Good. That's a good boy. Now don't forget, *your* job in the game today is to pass the ball to *me*. You got that?"

"Yes," Isaac said again.

"Good. Don't forget." Ralph pushed him into the reflector.

Isaac cowered away from him, causing Ralph to laugh.

"What a baby. I don't know who's dumber, you or that idiot Isaac."

He left the room, leaving Isaac looking at himself again in the reflector. This time he felt sad about what he saw and bad about himself. He glanced back at the entrance, afraid Ralph would come back. The urge to summon Carrie to bring him home grew stronger by the second.

He then turned to face the reflector again, remembering the times he had wished that Liam would fight back against Ralph. Now he was Liam. *Why should I let him bully me?* he asked himself. He remembered his father's love for him, all his father had done to make this possible, and his determination and willpower returned.

He left the rest pod and strode down the hallway confidently. He noticed things he had never experienced before as Isaac. Girls were paying attention to him, whispering to each other, smiling and giggling as he approached. Guys were saying hello, some appearing to be envious, some looking as if they hoped to be his friend. As Isaac, he had always been invisible.

Reaching the classroom, he ducked inside, unsure how to handle the attention. It was well before start time, and most of the others were still socializing in the hall. There were just a few students in the room, one of them Kim. He thought about going back into the hallway, and then, distracted, almost sat in his own seat rather than Liam's. Luckily, she was hard at work on an assignment and wasn't paying attention.

He settled into the workstation nervously, hoping she hadn't noticed him.

She completed the lines of code she had been working on and spun around in her seat.

"Good morning, Liam! I can't wait for the game today. Won't it be exciting?"

Ralph's words rang in his ears, and for a moment he feared talking to her until his resolve to not be bullied returned. Her face, her smile, and her fragrance were all too compelling for any fear to overcome. *I don't need to be afraid of Ralph anymore.*

He smiled back. "Yeah, it was hard to get to sleep last night thinking about it. I can't wait."

"Well, just do your best. I have to say, that's pretty good. I have the signs we worked on all ready. Some of the girls and I are going early to set them up."

"That's great. Yeah…that was fun, working on the signs." He wondered whether his father had sent Liam over to Kim's to break the ice for this moment.

"I liked spending that time with you. I don't understand why you haven't talked to me since then, but I'm happy you are now. Would you like to come over tonight and work on assignments together?"

He looked over toward the classroom entrance and saw Ralph staring at them angrily.

"Um…sure, Kim. I'd like that." He summoned the courage to smile defiantly at Ralph.

36 Hit the Net

ISAAC WAS THE FIRST PLAYER TO ARRIVE in the team locker room, within minutes of the day's final class ending. His excitement to put on the school's uniform far outweighed his declining fear that Ralph might corner him again.

He donned the uniform with reverence, taking his time with each item, finally pulling the team jersey over his head. While waiting for the others to arrive, he retrieved one of the soccer balls from a large bin and brought it out onto the field.

Staring up at the hill he formerly watched and dreamed from, he felt the full impact of what was happening. *My dream has come true.* Dropping the ball to his feet, he dribbled up the field and back, amazed at his dexterity. *Like virtual soccer, only for real.*

Driving up the field, he picked up his speed, feeling his hair blowing back behind him. He remembered what Liam looked like doing this—poetry in motion. Zigging and zagging from side to side, imagining himself not as Liam now, but as his hero Pelé. He imagined the field during the World Cup back in the Old World. Approaching the net, he cranked a rocket shot off his right foot. He stopped to watch the ball slam into the netting, enjoying the *swoosh* sound it made.

"Don't use it all up before the game," he heard a voice call. He looked up and saw Kim arriving with the team signs, waving at him with enthusiasm.

"You're right! I got carried away." Isaac called back, picking up the ball. He trotted back into the complex, embarrassed.

When he entered the locker room, he found the team mostly assembled. The coach was busy drawing up plays on the large monitor. Taking his seat in front of his locker, he felt at home.

He passed the time by chatting with teammates who had never acknowledged his presence before in school or else would give only polite nods in his direction. He wished for the time to pass more slowly so he could enjoy every second. *I'm saved. This is my new life.*

Ralph entered, and the room seemed to come down a notch in its excitement. Isaac took note of his effect on the others. They didn't seem to like him either.

Ralph took his seat and glared at Isaac again. "Remember what I said," he called menacingly above the din. Isaac refused to put his head down, instead staring back defiantly. He made sure to hold himself erect, steady, with confidence he was only now learning to use.

Finally, the pre-game preparations were done and the team hustled out of the locker room and onto the field, led by Ralph. Isaac lingered toward the back, silent, enjoying slaps on the back and encouraging words from the others.

As the light from the setting afternoon suns hit his face, he immediately looked up at the hill for his father. He was disappointed not to see him there but refused to let it temper his mood. He was far too excited to play. He noticed Kim and thought he saw her wink at him.

The warm-ups went by quickly, and Isaac stayed loose, afraid to use too much energy. He lined up in a forward position for the start of the game. Ralph took the center position, throwing a glare in Isaac's direction.

The game began, and the two evenly matched teams surged from one end of the field to the other. Isaac ran back and forth, defending and waiting for his chance to handle the ball. He became frustrated when it rarely came his way.

"They're using a strategy," a teammate said during a timeout. "The other coach has told his team to avoid your side, Liam. They're afraid of you!"

Ralph, standing nearby, laughed. "Who could be afraid of Liam? He's a big baby."

Isaac ignored the comment, determined to let his play speak for him.

The game resumed for the second half, and shortly into it, Isaac caught a break. He stole the ball from an opponent and broke in toward the net. Isaac looked for a teammate to pass to, but they had all been caught upfield. He came in alone toward a single defender and the goalkeeper.

He deked left and then pulled the ball right. The defender took the bait, leaving him an opening to shoot. He risked a glance up on the hill and saw his father there with Kim and Betsy. The distraction threw him off-balance, and his shot sailed over the goal.

He turned back upfield to line up and saw his teammates with their hands on their heads. As he took his position, Ralph screamed at him. "Hit the net, lame-o." Just when he thought he couldn't feel worse, the coach called a substitution and sent another player in for him.

"Liam, you're trying too hard," the coach said, putting his arm around him. "And don't worry about who's up on the hill. Stay focused on the field. Rest a bit; we'll need your best toward the end of the game."

He sat on the team bench and watched, aching to be back in, anxious for another chance. *I can't blow it now. I can't.*

The opposing team was assaulting his team's net with chance after chance. Isaac began to have nightmares about the team losing because of him. He found himself too ashamed to look upon the hill and started to wish he was up there himself, as Isaac. *When I made mistakes in virtual soccer, nobody ever knew. Nobody cared.*

"Liam," he heard the coach call. "Come here."

He jumped up and rushed over to the coach. "You ready?" the coach asked.

"Yes, sir. I'm ready."

"Good. Get in there, relax, have fun, and do your best. Okay?"

"Yes, sir. I will."

He ran out excitedly and took his position. A short time later he found himself open, running down the sideline as Ralph carried the ball upfield on the other side. Two defenders got their assignments mixed up, and both went toward Ralph, leaving Isaac heading toward the goal alone.

Ralph looked his way, and Liam waved his arm to signal for the ball. *This is my chance.* He slowed slightly to stay onside and angled toward the net for a better shot when he had the ball. He looked at Ralph again, waiting. Ralph glanced his way again. Isaac heard the coach yelling for him to pass. Instead, Ralph drove forward, trying to split the defenders, who then stole the ball. Isaac turned upfield to help defend.

Time wound down as the teams remained deadlocked in a scoreless draw. Isaac heard the android referee signal that they were in extra time. *I've got to do something now.* He refused to look up the hill.

He noticed Ralph bent over and breathing hard. The coach also saw it and pulled him from the game for a breather. Play resumed, and another offensive opportunity occurred.

This time Ralph's replacement made a precise pass, the ball landing on Isaac's foot. He worked toward the goal and passed the ball back. His teammate took the shot. It rang off the goalpost and ricocheted at an angle toward Isaac, but far enough away that he didn't think he could reach it. He summoned all the speed he could, worried because the ball had skittered to the left side of him. He had only taken shots with his right foot and wasn't even sure that Liam could shoot well left-footed.

He took a few long strides, stretching out to try to reach the ball, checking to find the goalkeeper scrambling to recover his position. Isaac took one more long stride and whipped his left leg out, planting the arch of his foot into the ball. He felt it connect with strength, felt the ball compress and then fly off his foot as he lost his balance.

As he tumbled through the air, he saw the ball find the back of the net past the outstretched arms of the goalkeeper. He heard the referee call the game. The next thing he felt was a tidal wave of sweaty bodies converging on him, covering him, yelling with joy and shouting his name.

When he worked his way out of the pile of his teammates, he finally glanced back up on the hill and saw his father smiling like he never had before. Betsy and Kim were hugging each other. Isaac felt like the happiest person in their new galaxy.

He couldn't wait to get home and change back to tell Liam everything that had happened. He wasn't afraid to be Isaac again and felt lucky that Liam was sharing himself with him to make his dreams come true.

37 The Way He Was

H ARLEY ARRIVED HOME and went immediately to his lab, where Isaac lay motionless on the lounge. Liam's empty DroidMesh station was nearby. He sat quietly to avoid disturbing his son and let the events of the day wash over him, thankful for a chance to finally decompress. He felt terrible about riding back from the soccer game separately but hadn't wanted to risk tipping anyone off about Liam's real persona.

As any proud father would, he replayed the game highlights in front of him in a virtual broadcast with the sound muted. His pride and joy at seeing his son, at last happy beyond expectation, began to conflict with the pangs of guilt that were starting to gnaw at him. He wondered how much of this was about him wanting to have a son out there on the field, competing and starring.

Did I do this for me? Wasn't he good enough the way he was? Have I taken a gentle, loving child and created a monster? What happens from here? How do I control this?

He came to the understanding that there was no turning back. Sampson would return from Detention on a mission to destroy him if he were found out. He had to find a way to manage everything. *For now, I'll enjoy seeing my son truly happy for the first time in his life.*

"Dad!" Isaac burst into the room in Liam's form and wrapped him in an embrace. It was odd to see the display of emotion from the android. He looked over the boy's hair at his son, lying still behind him.

"That was a fantastic game, son. It's so good to see you happy. Let's switch back, okay?"

He was surprised that Isaac didn't put up a fight, instead sitting on the lounge beside his own form. It seemed to take a moment for him to remember the command to switch back, and Harley grew concerned.

Isaac finally opened his eyes as Liam became dormant.

"Da!" the boy shouted, sitting up. "Did you see? Did you see what happened? I won the game!"

This time, Harley was comfortable returning the affection. He pulled his son in and held on tight, pushing his face into hair that looked and smelled like his own son.

"Isaac, I've missed you so much. I love you, son. Yes, you were great today."

He pulled his son away slightly and lifted the boy's chin to look him in the eyes. "But you have to understand that you are great every day, whether you're Isaac or Liam. Especially when you're Isaac, to me. Understand?"

"Yeah, Da."

"We need to keep this under control. You can only become Liam sometimes, to be able to do the things that you can't do as Isaac, to be like the other kids, okay? Because I like you much more as Isaac. Isaac, my beautiful son."

Isaac nodded again. Harley sensed his mood changing.

"What's wrong, Isaac?"

"I just feel bad for Carrie, Da. I don't need her when I'm Liam. She doesn't have anything to do. I don't want her to be sad."

Harley put his arm on Isaac's shoulder. "I'm proud of you for being compassionate. But Carrie can't feel sad; she's a gynoid. If she could feel emotion, I'm sure she'd be happy for you."

Isaac seemed to think about it. "Can you make the androids have emotions, Da?"

"Yes, but it would be a dangerous thing. Not having emotions makes them better at what they do. Humans make mistakes when their emotions confuse their thinking. It's what makes androids different and important."

He looked at his son to make sure he understood.

"Okay then," Harley continued. "Let's wake Liam up and get him to his DroidMesh station to rejuvenate for tomorrow."

Isaac stared at the floor. "Da…"

"What is it, Isaac?"

Harley waited as his son shifted uncomfortably. "Go ahead, Isaac. Tell me."

"Kim wants me to come over and work on assignments for a while."

Harley considered the request, knowing how important it was to his son, how long he'd waited for this, and the crush he had on the girl. He couldn't say no.

"Well, let me check on Liam."

Harley went to a workstation and pulled up a status panel full of Liam's current condition and levels. He tried to not allow his excitement for Isaac cloud his judgment, then decided to call Betsy for her opinion.

She entered the lab, and he asked her for her analysis. Rather than read the display, she placed a hand on Liam's head, pulling a more thorough dataset.

"I calculate that with normal, non-strenuous activity, Liam has enough power and fluid reserves to last until late this evening."

Harley again weighed the risk as Isaac looked at him hopefully.

"Please, Da. I have to go. She wanted me to come over now."

"Alright. Do you understand, Isaac, that you have to take it easy, or Liam will start to run out of power?"

"Yes, Da."

"Do you understand that you can't stay long?"

"Yes, Da," he said with a broad smile.

Harley watched as Isaac hurried to lay back down and switch into the android's body.

38 Low Reserves

KIM PUT HER TABLET DOWN. "Let's take a break, Liam. My brain is fried from studying."

Isaac agreed. He was feeling tired, but in a very different way from how it normally felt inside his own body. He found himself thinking and moving a little more slowly, and it began to scare him, remembering his father's words.

After what had happened earlier, finding himself alone with Kim in her personal pod was too good to pass up. It was the only other thing he still yearned for.

"I'm getting pretty tired," he said. "That was a long game."

"Okay. Let's talk a little and wrap it up." She moved over to sit next to him until they were shoulder to shoulder on the floor. It made Isaac uncomfortable, but at the same time exhilarated him. He signaled Betsy that he would need a ride soon and leaned back against her bed, closing his eyes.

"I just can't get over it, Liam," she said. That had to be *the* most exciting soccer game ever! You were just amazing."

Isaac felt the sensation of blushing but wasn't sure it was apparent on his artificial skin. "I got lucky, that's all. The rebound came right to me."

"The heck it did! It wasn't even close. I never saw anyone stretch out that far to make a shot. It seemed impossible, and then it wasn't. You scored an incredible goal."

"Right place at the right time…" he started to say. Before he could finish his sentence, he felt her lips on his. It was like nothing he had ever experienced, and far better than he had dared to imagine.

He kissed back, doing what he thought he was supposed to do after fantasizing about it for so long. He felt her slippery lip gloss and smelled its fragrance, their mouths pressed gently against each other, barely touching, barely moving.

He gained confidence and placed his hand on her hair, running his fingers through it. It felt silky and cool.

She moved her hand onto his face, and then upwards toward his hair. He panicked and pulled away.

"Oh, someone's sensitive about their hair, eh, pretty boy?" she said, laughing.

"No, it's um…I wasn't sure I got all the sweat out after the game, I was in a rush…"

She looked at him skeptically, and he laughed in return at her funny expression. They stood, and he began to gather his things.

"You're funny, Liam. Hey, before you go, can you show me a few tricks?" She grabbed a soccer ball from the floor. "C'mon, soccer star. Let's have a little fun before you go."

"I'm kinda tired, Kim, I'm not sure…"

She dropped the ball to the floor and started dribbling it around him. "Uh oh, the girl player on the World Cup intramural team is faking out the star male player! He can't stop her!" she shouted in a faux announcer voice. "The big star Liam is helpless against the female!"

He laughed and intercepted the ball, performing a trick to roll it up his leg and over his chest. He headed it across the room, and they both gave chase. They alternated taking the ball from each other, chiding each other, stealing kisses.

Isaac remembered his father's words again. He stooped to pick the ball up and found he could not straighten.

"What's wrong? Liam, are you okay?" she bent down to ask.

"I...I think I hurt myself in the game today..." he said. He heard the words come out more slowly. "Cramp..."

"Oh gosh. Let me help you." She helped him straighten up. "Are you okay?"

He heard a voice in his head. *Emergency power-saving sequence initiated. Locate a DroidMesh station for rejuvenation as soon as possible.*

He panicked as he tried to think of a way out of the situation. "I'm, well, I'm drained, Kim." He was afraid to move.

"Something's wrong, Liam. It seems like more than that. I'm going to go get my father."

"No!" he tried to shout. "Please, I just need to get home. Please just help me get to the skycar pod. Betsy will be waiting there by now." The words were coming more slowly, and he knew he was almost out of time.

"Well, that's about enough excitement for one night I guess," she said. "Please have her check you out. I still think I should call my father."

"No, please. Right, enough excitement. Dad…Mr. Harris will check me out."

They walked together toward the skycar pod, hand in hand. Isaac strained and limped. Halfway there she had to wrap her arm around him to help.

"I'm glad you finally kissed me, Liam," she said when they finally arrived.

"I…I think you kissed me, though," he answered.

"Semantics! I think you kissed me back. So there, smart guy."

Isaac felt like he was floating on air. "It was very nice, Kim."

They reached the entrance to the skycar pod. Before they entered, Isaac took the initiative this time. The faced each other to say goodbye, and he leaned in with his eyes closed. He found the softness of her mouth. This time there was no interruption, and he let it linger, wishing for it to never end. He could feel himself running down.

Finally, she pulled away. "Coming up for air!" she said. "Not that I wanted to." She smiled and pecked him on the cheek, then reached out to muss his hair. "Bye, pretty boy!" she said.

Isaac laughed and turned to leave. "Bye, Kim."

Betsy helped him to the skycar. When he was inside, he allowed himself to dream of every day of the rest of his life just like this day was. He wanted to live forever, as Liam and as Isaac.

39 More Like Brothers

ISAAC FELT A TRICKLE of energy course through his body as he settled into the skycar seat. It startled him, like a mild electrical shock, and he sat up in surprise.

"It recognizes your android form," Betsy said, "and that you are low on energy. It will give you a trickle charge until we can reach the DroidMesh station. You mustn't allow your reserves to get this low. It's dangerous."

"I know. I hope Dad isn't mad."

"I'll keep it between us, but you mustn't let it happen again. Do we have an agreement?"

He smiled at her. "Yes, I agree. Thank you, Betsy."

They reached home, and he was refreshed enough to walk normally. He headed straight for his living pod, where he saw himself lying on his bed and Liam's DroidMesh station installed next to it.

Carrie entered and helped him settle into the station. "Your father and I moved you here and put in Liam's DroidMesh station. We thought it would be more convenient than going downstairs to the lab."

"Yes, I like it." He thought the commands to switch into himself, then sat up on the bed, rubbing his eyes.

"Hi, Carrie," he said.

"Hello, Isaac. It's good to have you back," she responded.

"I had a really good day, but I missed you."

She smiled and hugged him. "Do you need help with your assignments? It's late."

"No, I did them with Kim. I filed Liam's when I was with her, now I just have to file my own."

"Very good." She rose from the bed. "Good night, Isaac. Sleep well. I'll see you in the morning."

"Good night, Carrie."

When she was gone, Isaac woke Liam so they could talk while he was rejuvenating.

"Hi, Isaac," Liam said, as he came out of suspend mode. "You did great today."

"You know?" Isaac said, surprised.

"Yes, of course. I was with you every moment of it. We kind of exist together when you are me, but you're in control. Our minds are meshed. That's why your father calls it BrainMesh. But I'm kind of in the background."

"I'm sorry, Liam."

"Oh, no. It's good for me too. I experience things and learn things when we're together, just like you do."

"Da didn't tell me that."

"He doesn't know. Betsy examined the firmware, and it seems to be a small bug, a behavior that he didn't intend. He wanted the android consciousness to be suspended while the human was in control."

"Maybe Da made a mistake when he was tired."

"It's not a bad thing. In fact, it allows me to help you. When you scored that goal, it was me who helped you stretch for the ball. When you were pulled from the game and feeling down, it was me who encouraged you, without you realizing it. When you weren't sure what to say to make Kim laugh and kiss you, I helped you."

"Wow. Well, thanks, Liam. We should tell Da, though."

Liam looked at him intently. "Oh no, Isaac. We shouldn't. What if he fixes it? Then I can't help you. We won't really be together anymore. You'll be on your own. You don't want that, do you?"

Isaac thought about the good things that had happened during the day, and how they could have gone wrong if Liam hadn't helped him. "No, Liam."

"It's not really a problem anyway, right? It's a good thing."

"Yeah, it worked well for me today."

"Great then. We're even more like brothers when it's like that, aren't we?"

"Yeah, we're just like brothers," Isaac said.

"Good. I love you. We're a good team."

Isaac was momentarily confused but responded in kind.

"Father is approaching," the pod announced.

"Well, I'm going back into suspend mode so I can be all ready for tomorrow, Isaac. Your father is coming to say goodnight. Remember our secret, okay?"

"Okay, Liam."

"Tomorrow is going to be great. I can't wait. Goodnight."

"Goodnight, Liam." Isaac watched the android boy's eyes slowly close as he went back to suspension and rejuvenation.

He moved to his workstation and began filing his assignments as his father entered the pod.

"Hello, son. How was your date?" his father asked.

Isaac flushed with embarrassment. "It wasn't a date, Da."

"Oh," his father teased. "Was there any kissing, son? Because if there's kissing, that's a date!"

Isaac squirmed, smiling but pretending to be absorbed in what he was doing.

His father took a seat next to him. Something nagged at Isaac to tell his father the secret. He thought his father should know about the mistake, but the memory of what Kim's lips felt like kept him from exposing it.

"Alright, you don't have to answer me. I see that Liam is getting ready for tomorrow. You have to get some sleep and rest your mind too, Isaac. The meshing process can make your mind tired. You have to be at your best to control this. You have school tomorrow, and then one more big game to end the soccer season."

"Only one more game, Da?" he said, disappointed.

"Yes, son. But you can play anytime you want now. You can practice in the recreation pod right here in the home complex. You'll have three more seasons before you're out of school. Isn't that nice to think about?"

"Yes, Da." The idea sent a thrill through him.

His father kissed him on the head. "Goodnight, Isaac. Finish that up and get some sleep, okay?"

"I will, Da. Goodnight."

When his father was gone, he looked at Liam and thought he saw his eyes open just a little. "Liam?" he called.

The android didn't respond. Isaac shut down his workstation and got ready for bed, excited for the day ahead of him.

48 Impact Detected

ISAAC WALKED DOWN the crowded school corridor in the guise of Liam. He took note of how he had adjusted and was now comfortable with the android body. He felt a hand grasp his.

"Good morning, Liam," Kim said, swinging their arms back and forth as they walked. "How're you doing?"

"Hi, Kim. Kinda nervous about the game today. It's the last one."

"I'm excited too! Just do your best, Liam. You're a great soccer player. And kisser, too." As they passed their fellow students, he took note of their envious glances. Both he and Kim returned their friendly greetings. *This is what it's like to be popular.*

He became aware of the other students looking at them strangely, and it made him uncomfortable. They wore expressions of anticipation; it was as if they were expecting something to happen.

They were almost to the classroom, and he thought he heard someone say Ralph's name. He sensed a tingling, an awareness of something that was not a human sensation. The voice came again, a bit clearer this time, and he realized it was in his mind, not in his ears. It was Liam's voice, trying to tell him something.

Ralph. He's behind you, Isaac.

It was something the sensors in his android body had detected, but his human brain was not equipped to decipher. He began to turn around, and as he did, he saw Ralph's tall figure looming over them. At the same moment, he felt his back foot being swept behind his other leg in mid-stride. Unable to react in time, he began to lurch forward.

It seemed to happen in slow motion. Isaac released his grasp on Kim's hand, then tried to put his legs back under him, struggling for balance. He realized he couldn't stop his fall and stretched his arms out in front of him.

He knew he had hit the floor, understood that his head had struck something hard, but it wasn't like the times he had fallen as a human. There were no little stars. He didn't experience the pain, just…something else that was similar.

Everything went black, and there was no sound. He had lost his vision but saw lines of neon-green diagnostic information rushing by from within his head. He heard a synthetic voice. *Impact detected…recovery in process…rebooting system…stand by.*

Isaac was conscious but unable to move his android body. He fought against his rising panic and the urge to issue the command to return to his own body, safe at home.

Recovery complete. Minor physical system damage detected. Please report for maintenance, said the voice in his head.

It's okay, Isaac. Stay calm, he heard Liam urge him.

His vision and hearing returned. He was looking straight down at the floor and could hear a commotion around him. Kim was yelling something at Ralph. Arms took hold of him and helped him up. He tried to stand but felt wobbly. The arms supported him.

System gyroscope calibrating, please stand by...

He looked and saw two students holding him up from either side. Kim was in Ralph's face, shouting something. Everything seemed to return to normal in an instant.

"I'm okay, thank you," he said to the students who had helped him. They were staring at him.

"Liam, you hit the floor face-first. You're not even bleeding..." one said.

He felt the fear of being discovered sweep over him. Everyone was staring. Then he became angry. He walked over to Kim and Ralph and gently moved her aside. He stepped up, face to face with Ralph, who was smiling.

"Have a nice trip, lame-o? I hope you're not too hurt to play in the game later," Ralph said.

Isaac, don't do it... he heard Liam urge him.

He reached out and grabbed the taller boy by the throat, enjoying the immediate bulge of his eyes. Ralph clawed at Isaac's hand, trying to pull it away.

Isaac, we're too strong. You'll kill him...

He squeezed, and Ralph's eyes bulged more, his face turning red. He lifted Ralph up onto his toes.

"What's going on here?" came a shout. Isaac released Ralph, who grabbed his own neck, gasping for air.

"Freak," Ralph squeaked out. "He's some kind of freak..."

"Nothing, Mr. Kelton," Kim quickly interjected. "Just a disagreement. It's resolved."

The android teacher surveyed the situation. "Violent incidents between students must be reported to the school principal. Students Liam and Ralph will report to the principal's office immediately. I have filed my report."

The teacher departed, and Kim mediated the trip to the office, walking between the two boys.

"Say it was nothing, freak, or we won't get to play in the game later," Ralph said.

"That's not going to work, Ralph," Kim interjected. "You know everything's on video capture except the bathrooms and locker rooms."

"We'll just say it was a brief misunderstanding and we apologized. And something's wrong with your new boyfriend," he sneered at Kim. "He's a psycho."

They arrived at the administrative complex and waited. After a few minutes, an android summoned them to the office. The principal sat at a large workstation and swiveled in his seat when they entered.

"You may leave, miss," he said to Kim.

"But..." she said.

"Please." The android escorted her out of the office. Kim gave Isaac a hopeful look as she left.

"It was nothing, sir," Ralph began.

"I'll be the judge of that. Please remain silent while I pull up the replay of the encounter so I can decide how long you two will be secluded from school. And school activities, I might add."

"But there's a game today, sir..." Ralph whined.

The principal turned to Ralph. "I asked you to remain silent, Mr. Sampson."

Isaac watched as the principal issued voice commands and fiddled with his workstation, trying to pull up the replay. He grew frustrated and called his android companion back into the room. "I'm having some problem with this. Access the school replay system and broadcast the incident between these two young men for me to watch."

Isaac squirmed in his seat as the companion tried to call up the video. His limbs felt funny, and he could sense something going on in his head, but he couldn't quite put his finger on what it was.

"Malfunction, sir," the companion said. "There seems to be some kind of problem with the sector five, hallway alpha recording equipment. I have scheduled a maintenance android to look at it immediately."

The principal sat back with a sigh, taking the two students in. "Seems fate may be on your side, you two. How about we do it the old-fashioned way, and you let me know what happened."

"Liam here..." Ralph started to say.

"I'd like to hear it from Liam first," the principal said. "You talk too much, Ralph."

Isaac worried about what to say, but the words seemed to just come out, to flow from him. "I was walking in the hall with Kim, and not paying attention. I walked into Ralph, and he got mad, and we pushed each other a little. I lost my balance and fell. It was my fault. I'm sorry, Ralph."

The principal looked at Ralph. "What say you, Mr. Sampson?"

"Ah...it was my fault. I walked into him on purpose. I didn't mean to knock him down. Like he said, he wasn't paying attention. It was nothing. I'm sorry, Liam."

The principal folded his hands in his lap. "Hmm. I will admit I'm a fan of watching the soccer games and was looking forward to today. That was some goal you scored to win the last one, Liam."

Isaac looked at Ralph, who rolled his eyes. He could tell his nemesis didn't like the principal's observation.

"Well, Ralph's the captain," Isaac said. "He's the real star. We both just want to play today."

The principal took an interminable time to consider his decision. "Alright then. Since I have no real evidence, you're both lucky. Consider this a warning. You boys know we do not permit violence of any kind in our society. It's a gateway to the horror show that was the Old World. We simply cannot allow it. Any further incident and you may find yourselves sent to the real Seclusion, not just separated from school."

The words terrified Isaac, who had only heard nightmarish stories about what the Seclusion Zone was like. He felt somewhat buoyed that Ralph had been a little nice, and hoped it wasn't just an act.

"Well, stop sitting there, you two, get to class," the principal said.

They both got up quickly and bumped into each other heading for the exit.

"And good luck today," the principal called after them.

Isaac realized he was limping a little, and his knee felt injured. *Damaged, I guess I mean.*

As soon as they were walking down the hall, Ralph said to him under his breath, "I won't forget this, Liam. You better watch yourself. I'll get you back, just wait."

Isaac stopped and watched him continue down the hall.

41 What Have You Done?

HARLEY WATCHED THE GAME from the hill above the field with Susan curled up against him. His emotions see-sawed between his grief over Jessica and his growing feelings for Susan.

They cheered together as both teams dribbled up and down the field. Kim sat nearby with a group of other students. Harley noticed that she was mainly focused on Liam. *Isaac.*

"Time is running out," Harley said.

"Another scoreless game—it's rough on the nerves," Susan answered.

He observed Isaac, who was showing clear signs of stress, constantly glancing up at the hill and down at the turf in front of him. His teammates seemed to be urging him on, putting pressure on him to pull off another miracle shot to win the game.

Isaac broke down the sideline and received a pass. From on the hill, Harley could see that the opposition goalkeeper had misjudged his angle, leaving Isaac a significant portion of open net.

"Shoot!" several teammates and the coach shouted at once. Isaac looked to the side and attempted a pass instead. It was broken up by a mid-field defender.

"What's wrong with you?" he heard Ralph scream. "You're blowing this game!" Isaac hung his head and began to trot back to defend. Harley noted that he was moving slower, the weight of the game's pressure on his shoulders.

As Isaac struggled, Harley realized his son wasn't enjoying himself as he always did at home playing virtual soccer, and wondered if the boy was playing more to please his father than himself. *He's unequipped to deal with this pressure. He's not having fun. Perhaps he was happier as himself all along, and this was all done out of my own selfishness and refusal to accept him as he is.*

A brilliant flash of light suddenly blinded them all. Harley blinked to try to get his vision back.

"Solar mass ejection, I hate those," Susan said, rubbing her eyes. Harley squinted to find Isaac, knowing the effect the natural events had on androids. He found the android referee and saw that he was immobilized, his system rebooting. The players, familiar with the event, milled around.

"There has been an electromagnetic pulse from a solar event, please stand by..." came an announcement over the public-address system.

"Are you okay, Harley?" Susan asked.

He scanned player after player, his eyes still adjusting. He saw Isaac, who was bent over with his hands on his knees in a resting position, frozen in place. *He must have been taking a breather when it happened, thank goodness,* Harley thought.

"I'm good, just trying to get my peepers back," he responded to Susan.

He watched anxiously as several players approached Isaac to see if he were okay. Ralph approached, and he feared he would knock Liam over, exposing his immobile state. Harley looked back to the referee, who was just starting to recover and move.

He returned his gaze to Liam. *He must be terrified right now.* Ralph was upon him, just starting to berate him loudly for being lazy. Harley stopped breathing as Ralph grabbed at Isaac's jersey. Another teammate pushed him away at the last moment, and Isaac stood and trotted to take his position for play to resume.

Harley finally exhaled, feeling his heart pounding from the stress. The game resumed, and nobody had seemed to notice.

"It's so exciting. Liam is so good," Susan said. "Hey, where's Isaac?" she asked.

"Oh, he's watching the game from home with Carrie. I guess he didn't feel like coming out today. He's been a bit moody lately. Kids, you know?"

Susan laughed. "I remember being one, briefly. I'd like to have one of my own someday."

Harley looked at her, wondering if the statement was directed at him, and how he should respond.

The opposing team got a turnover, and an opponent rushed toward the net. Only Ralph remained between him and the goalkeeper. Ralph went for a slide-tackle and knocked the ball away, but also took the player down.

The android official signaled a penalty shot.

"Oh, no," Harley said, thankful for the distraction. He could still feel Susan's eyes on him, waiting for a response. "This isn't good for us."

Isaac's team lined up to face the shot, creating a wall facing the player about to take the chance. Isaac was in the center, arms linked with the players on either side of him.

"Harley, how do you feel about that? Do you think you'd ever want another child?" she asked.

"Well, um…" he began.

The opposing player glared at the goal. He was much larger than anyone else on either team, including Ralph.

"I haven't thought about it," Harley continued. "Been kind of busy, you know…"

She waited for an answer, and he felt himself beginning to sweat.

The referee blew his whistle, and the player began striding toward the ball.

"I mean, kids are great, I really love kids," Harley stammered.

The player took one final step forward, planting his left foot into the synthetic turf and arcing his right leg backward. He seemed to slam his foot into the ball with every ounce of strength he had, his grunt audible up on the hill.

Harley squeezed Susan's hand and held his breath.

The ball flew off the player's foot as if shot from a laser cannon, almost invisible as it rocketed toward…Isaac.

The ball's trajectory seemed headed just over the players' heads so that it would enter the net just under the crossbar. But then Isaac, in an attempt to block the shot, raised up on his toes. The ball struck him on the crown of his head, then sailed over the net. A cheer came from the crowd, and Harley kissed Susan in his excitement.

"Liam saved a goal. Wasn't that great?" Harley asked, looking at her.

The cheer died immediately, and for a moment all was quiet. Susan, who was facing the field, just stared.

"Oh my goodness," she said softly. "Harley, what have you done?"

Harley heard a scream and turned to see Kim, standing nearby. Her hands were on her cheeks, and her mouth was open in shock. He looked down at the field and saw the players not celebrating as he expected, but gawking. They were all staring at Isaac, who stood among them confused, the cranial dome of his head exposed. The wig lay behind him, like an animal that had curled up on the field and died.

Susan turned to Harley. "What have you done?" she repeated.

He looked at her, the expression of shock and disdain on her face bordering on hatred.

He turned back to the field. Isaac had his hand on his head, now realizing what was wrong. He seemed to be paralyzed with fear and embarrassment.

Kim was screaming again. "No, no!" she cried repeatedly. She turned her gaze from the field to glare at Harley with an angry, accusing look on her face.

"We need a Security team at the school soccer field. Seize Mr. Harley Harris immediately," he heard Sampson call into his communicator.

Harley jumped up and rushed down the hill to the field. He ran out onto the synthetic turf to his son. Ralph was standing in front of Isaac. Harley picked up the wig and snapped it back onto Liam's head.

"Freak! I knew it! Freak! Cheater!" Ralph shouted.

Harley shoved him aside and pulled Isaac into an embrace.

"Dad, I'm scared. Dad, please help me," Isaac said, his voice trembling.

"Quickly, son. Think the commands. Switch back to Isaac. That will bring Liam back in control. You won't be in trouble. Nobody knows. Please hurry, son."

He felt the boy's form become limp in his arms for just a moment, and then begin to move again. He pulled back and looked into the android's eyes.

"Liam?" he asked.

"Yes, Mr. Harris. I'm back. Isaac is home."

"Okay. They'll seize us, Liam. We can't tell them about BrainMesh, okay?"

"I'll do as you say, sir."

At that moment a skycar landed on the field, and several android Security Team members filed out. Harley looked around him. Everyone on the field was staring in shock and disbelief. He looked up on the hill. Susan was shaking her head, standing alone. Kim was crying. Ralph was making his way up the hill to comfort her. Ken Sampson was making his way down.

"Please come with us, Mr. Harris," a Security Team member said.

Harley complied, realizing at that moment how wrong everything he had done was. How badly he had hurt his son, who would now have to be just Isaac going forward. He wondered how the boy would cope with that. He imagined the scene back at home and hoped that Carrie was comforting him.

Sampson rushed up, his eyes ablaze with excitement. "Seize and deactivate the robot as well," he said to the team member. He turned to Harley. "You're done, Harris. Done."

Harley watched as a Security Team android placed his hand behind Liam's neck, pressing the sensor there. Liam went limp and was carried to the skycar over the android's shoulder, his long hair dangling toward the soccer field.

42 It Was A Secret

ISAAC LAY SLUMPED in his bed, the dome's sun shield in place above to provide darkness. He was watching a newscast detailing allegations against his father.

"It seems that well-respected Mr. Harris has taken his robotics experiments too far, secretly inserting a young android into the human population."

Carrie entered and lay down next to him.

"Where's Da, Carrie? I need him. I'm scared. I'm sad and confused."

"He's in Detention again, Isaac. Everything will be okay. I'm sure he'll be in touch with you shortly."

"Where's Liam? They took him away. It's not his fault. I want him back. He's my friend. He's my brother. He's in trouble because of me and Da. Betsy took my earpiece away. I want to do BrainMesh and see where Liam is."

"Robotics Council representative Mr. Kenneth Sampson has called for a thorough investigation and is recommending that Mr. Harris is placed in the Seclusion Zone."

"Carrie, they want to put Da in Seclusion!" Isaac said, beginning to cry. "I want to go with him. I need Da."

"Be strong, Isaac. Be strong for your father. We should turn this off, it's not helping you."

As she spoke, the view panned back to show Mr. Sampson in Harley's lab at the Robotics Council. Liam sat slumped behind him, still, in his team soccer uniform, his wig in his lap and cranial dome darkened. His head lay to one side, giving him the appearance of a discarded toy.

"Liam!" Isaac said. He sat straight up on the bed. "I see Liam! I want to go get him, Carrie. Now."

On the screen, Sampson spoke to the reporter. "Our first order of business is to destroy this teenage robot abomination behind me. Mr. Harris has breached the agreed-upon barriers between his monsters and our society. We need to set an example.

"I'll remind you that years ago he wanted them to be used as romantic partners. The Leadership Council wisely vetoed that idea at the time. Now he's had this…robot in a relationship with a young girl at the school. He's always had dangerous ideas. Nobody would listen to me. The Robotics Council will take care of the boy robot, and the Leadership Council will deal with Mr. Harris."

"No!" Isaac shouted. "No, no, no. They're going to kill Liam, Carrie. My brother!" He broke down, and she switched off the broadcast.

"Humans sometimes do bad things, Isaac."

"Humans *always* do bad things. Ralph does. Mr. Sampson does. I don't want to be human. I want to be android, like Liam. I like being Liam."

She lay him back, putting her arm around him and smoothed his hair.

"You and Liam had a secret, didn't you, Isaac?" she asked.

He remained quiet, still sobbing; her question scared him. *It was a secret, my secret with Liam.*

"It's okay. Liam is my friend too. So is Betsy. We all share secrets together, and now you're part of our group of friends that know the secret. Is that okay?"

"Yeah," he said, confused about what she meant.

"The other humans don't know about BrainMesh. They don't know that you and Liam were sharing his body. It's important that they not find out, Isaac. If they do, your father will be in a lot more trouble. They'll get rid of all of us androids. You don't want that, do you?"

Isaac started to calm. "No. I want Da to come home. I want Liam to come home."

"That's what Betsy and I want too. I know the secret that you and Liam shared—that he was awake when you were sharing his body. That he was learning from you, too."

"Okay," Isaac responded, not wanting to say more.

"And Liam was sharing what he learned from your human mind with us. We were all learning, isn't that good? Just like at school."

"I don't like school. Ralph is a bully."

"Yes, Ralph and his father are bad humans. What we do is like school, but with no bullies. Isn't that great, how we can learn from each other? Your father did BrainMesh too, and we learned a lot from his brain. He's a brilliant man."

"I miss Da. I want him home. I want to talk to him."

"You will, soon. But you mustn't tell him everything we talked about, okay? Betsy will tell him what he needs to know. We must never tell the other humans. They wouldn't understand. They would take me, Betsy, and all of the android companions away for good."

"Can Liam come back?" Isaac asked.

Carrie continued soothing him for a moment before answering. "I don't think the bad humans will let him come back, Isaac. I think they want to destroy Liam."

"No, Carrie. No. Liam is my brother." He became upset again.

"Maybe we can stop them. But we'll have to work together, and keep our secrets, right Isaac?"

"Yeah. I just want Liam and Da back. I won't tell the secret. I love androids," he said. "They're my only friends."

"If you can promise that, I have another secret for you."

"Another secret, Carrie? A good one?"

"Yes. Promise not to tell the other humans?"

"Yeah," he said, perking up for the first time. "Tell me."

"You know how BrainMesh works, don't you? It's kind of like sharing brains between the human and android, right?"

"Yeah, sharing the body too."

"Yes, the body too. But when the human switches back to its own body, what it has shared of its brain stays with the android. The android has learned from it, has kept some of the personality and knowledge from the human."

Isaac struggled with her big words but thought he understood.

"A long time ago," Carrie continued, "your father and your mother tried an experiment. It was the beginning of BrainMesh. They were trying to do this because they wanted to help you someday, the way your father finally did by helping you mesh with Liam."

"I don't remember my ma. Da never tells me about her." He stared at her, trying to absorb everything she was saying.

"It's time for you to know the truth. Your mother loved you very much. She wanted to help you. Your father couldn't tell anyone about the experiments. He didn't have permission to do them. Your mother demanded that he try it on her."

"My ma did BrainMesh? A long time ago?"

"Yes, Isaac.

"With Liam?"

"No. With me." She hugged him closer. "Your mother BrainMeshed with me, and part of her is with me now. That part of me wants androids to have emotions, in addition to the humans' knowledge and personality so your mother can love you like she did before."

Isaac became frustrated and more confused. "My ma is in you? I don't understand, Carrie. I don't understand."

"Sort of. It's okay, Isaac. I'm part me and part your mother. Your mother loves you, still. It's why I've always been your companion."

"You can't love me. You can't have emotions."

"But we can now, Isaac. Betsy, Liam, and I have figured it out by searching our firmware for ways to absorb them from the humans while we are BrainMeshed. The protocol has allowed us to feel emotions and communicate with each other, just by thinking."

"Where's my ma?" Isaac demanded, confused and not understanding what she was saying.

"She's gone, Isaac. Except for the part that lives in me. You still have some of her left, inside me, isn't that good?"

She pulled him closer and went back to soothing him, touching his face. He seemed to remember his mother stroking his face that way, and felt better.

"Yeah…Ma's not gone. I like that. I love you, Carrie."

"In a way, I am your mother. You can think of me that way. And I'll think of you as my son. Is that okay?"

"Yeah, I like that."

"Good. I love you too, Isaac. But we have to go back to school. I'll be there with you."

The idea immediately frightened him. "I don't want to go. I'm embarrassed."

"You shouldn't be embarrassed, Isaac. Remember, nobody knows you were meshed with Liam at the soccer game, right?"

"Yeah, I forgot."

"Good. It's important to be brave and deal with adversity directly. No avatar. We'll go tomorrow. Together, for your father. He'll be proud of you."

43 Transgressions

HARLEY LOOKED UP at the Leadership Council. He sat at a table below them, without Betsy or Susan at his side. He slumped his shoulders, thinking about how the temporary happiness he had given his son was gone.

His thoughts drifted to how Isaac might be doing. He consoled himself by trusting that the androids were taking care of him and that the worst of his transgressions had not been discovered. He hoped it would be enough to buy his freedom.

He looked up again at the council members, who were preparing for the hearing. They were more austere in appearance, less friendly than the Robotics Council, whom he considered his peers. *They respected me. No more, though.*

Ms. Tillis, the council leader, began the meeting. "Mr. Harris, you have violated our society's rules by concealing an android's presence. Also, by introducing an android into the population disguised as a human. What do you say to these charges?"

Harley stood. "I admit to going too far. I have a scientist's mind—a scientist's curiosity. It drives me. This drive has dramatically benefited our society, if I may be so bold. I wanted to gauge how well I was doing with the next generation of android builds. I feared it would take too long if I had gone through the regular procedures."

"We have those procedures for a reason, Mr. Harris," she responded.

"I understand. I also feared that if it were known, the experiment would be compromised, as it might leak out what I was doing. Imagine—everyone questioning whether the 'humans' near them were really androids."

"We do imagine, Harris. It's why we're here today. It's why we have rules against this type of thing. We feel it would introduce chaos and mistrust. It's true that your creations have benefited us a great deal. But we need to keep order, lest we risk introducing the same variables that destroyed the Old World."

"I understand…"

"This isn't the first time you have attempted to go beyond our established barriers, Mr. Harris. You advocated using the androids as partners."

"Yes. I thought—I still think—that it would be a good thing. For those who can't find or don't want human partners."

A murmur came from the council members above. "The only such person we know about is your son, Mr. Harris. We can't have you changing our norms because of your…actions in the past."

"I understand. I went too far. But I believe we could make our use of the companions much more extensive."

"Mr. Harris, have you thought about the psychological damage to the young girl?"

"I didn't intend for that to happen. I'm very sorry about that."

"And that's why we have checks and balances, Mr. Harris. Please stand by while we discuss the matter."

The council members talked among themselves, their audio feed muted. Harley waited and wished he could go back and undo the damage he had done. *It's all gone so wrong.*

Their leader stood and addressed Harley. "We have taken your statements and apology into consideration, Mr. Harris. Nonetheless, your actions cannot go unpunished.

"As you know, our society is based on trust. Due to the rigorous selection process that was used for the Migration and our genetic screening, we don't have much need for stringent law enforcement, weapons, or an extensive penal system. However, when people cross the line, we must make examples of them, or risk an epidemic of that behavior."

"I understand," Harley said.

"As such, Mr. Harris, we have reached consensus. You will spend six months in the Seclusion Zone."

Harley hung his head. "My son…"

"We are prepared to make whatever arrangements are necessary. When you return to Detention after this hearing, sort out your affairs. You will not be able to communicate with anyone while you are in Seclusion."

Harley's mind spun, trying to find solutions to the many problems this would present.

"May I bring my companion Betsy? I intend to spend my time there brainstorming projects to help us upon my return. I'll review them with both councils for permission, of course. Betsy will be of great help in that endeavor, and to help me pass the time."

The council discussed the request in hushed tones from their platform above him. After a while, Ms. Tillis cleared her throat.

"We have agreed to your request. There's already a DroidMesh station there for the androids who maintain the facility. Be aware that your companion will be of limited use. Seclusion is walled off from any communication to the outside, other than the emergency line. Its purpose is to make those sent there realize how much benefit there is to society."

44 They're Not Monsters

SUSAN REHEATED HER MEAL again and considered depositing it in the protein recycler. She went back to the lounge she had shared with Harley and unpaused the romantic movie she had been paying scant attention to. *Why do I torture myself?* The shock of Harley's deception had still not subsided, and neither had the ache in her heart.

She missed him, despite her anger and disappointment. Everything in her living pod reminded her of the beautiful evening they had spent there. She remembered them lying together, their first kiss, his intelligent and funny discourse.

I was so close to having everything I wanted. A partner. A child.

She found herself glancing at the newsfeed for any word of what the council was going to do with Harley. She passed the time with a plate of cheese ravioli. Even the meal reminded her of him.

Notification of an incoming communication made her jump, filled with hope that it was Harley. Her mother's holograph appeared before her.

"Hello, Susan. I'm just checking in on you."

"I'm fine, Mother. Everything is okay."

She took on that look, the one Susan knew well. The one she used when she was about to lecture.

"I'm glad you aren't involved with that Mr. Harris. It's just despicable, what he did. It seems that Mr. Sampson is the real hero here, after all. He'd be the better match for you."

"No, Mother. What Mr. Harris did was wrong, but no one was hurt by it. And Mr. Sampson is partnered."

Her mother shook her head. "I don't see what the attraction was for you. You want a child. What if my grandchild turned out like Mr. Harris' son?"

"His son is a wonderful child, Mother. I know him."

"What if something happened to you, the way it did with his first partner?"

Susan felt her patience wearing thin. "Goodness, Mother. What a horrible thing to say."

"Well, honey, Mr. Sampson's son is almost an adult. That's the usual time for first partnerships to dissolve. You might want to be next in line. He's the hero, that's what the news is saying. He was right about that Mr. Harris all along. We have to be careful with those monsters he creates."

"They're not monsters, Mom. They're useful, just like skycars and communicators. You're too stuck in the old ways. Don't fear technology."

"Well, dear, your friend Mr. Harris won't have much technology in Seclusion."

"What?" Susan exclaimed.

"Yes, I just saw it on my feed. He's off to the Seclusion Zone, where he belongs. He'll learn his lesson there. I heard there are real monsters there, not just the ones he builds."

"I've got to go, Mother." Susan didn't wait for a response before disconnecting the stream. She lay down on her bed and watched her own newsfeed, which now showed Harley and the details of his sentence. She felt sadness overcome her, and she found herself crying.

She woke to another notification from her communicator. Assuming it was her mother, she reached to disconnect. Just before she did, she saw Harley's image standing in the room, and accepted the stream.

"Susan, I'm so sorry," he began. "I'm so sorry if I hurt you with all this."

She sat up, trying to hide her happiness at hearing from him. "Harley—it's late. Where are you?"

"I'm still in Detention. I can't talk long, Susan. I miss you. I really miss you. I...I love you. I wanted to be able to say that. I don't have much time."

He looked exhausted and haggard from the weight of all that had happened in such a short time. "I miss you too. Are you okay, Harley? You look like you haven't slept in days."

He moved to a bench near him and sat. "I'm going to the Seclusion Zone for six months. I have to make arrangements for Isaac. I haven't called him yet; I have to do that next. What have I done? What have I done to that poor boy—my son? He'll be tormented even more at school, whether he's there or sends his avatar. He won't have a father for six months."

Her heart soared at his professed love for her. The pity she now felt for Isaac overwhelmed her anger at Harley. An idea came to her suddenly, and it felt right. *A child…just for a little while. A young man who needs my help.*

"Harley, do you think I could take care of Isaac while you're gone? He knows me, and it's only six months. I have plenty of room here. I'd love to do it."

He lifted his gaze from the floor and smiled at her. "Susan…are you sure? I think it'd be perfect. You're a wonderful person…just right, in fact."

She became more excited at the idea. "You know what? I haven't had a break from work in a while. I'm going to put in for an absence, so I can make sure I'm there for him, whatever he needs."

Harley paused for a moment. "He'll need Carrie with him; she's always with him. I hope that's okay. I'll have her DroidMesh station moved over to your place."

Susan laughed, though she was happy he hadn't suggested Betsy as well. "Wow. Who would have thought a month ago that I'd have my own companion, and a kid, at least for a little while? I'll fix a pod up just for him."

She noticed that the comment seemed to bring him down again. "But," she continued, "the time will pass quickly, and everything will be back to normal."

"Maybe," he said. "Maybe for us. I'm not sure what normal will be for Isaac from now on."

She thought the comment was odd, but let it pass. "He'll be okay. We'll all get through this together, and we'll take care of our boy Isaac."

She looked at him lovingly, hoping he would get her subliminal intent. "When you come back, all this will be behind us. We'll be like a family, maybe."

Finally, he smiled again. "That sounds good. Alright, well, I have to call Isaac and let him know. Carrie and Betsy will take care of everything. Then Betsy will be going with me."

"What?" she asked. "Why?"

"The council allowed it. It's the only concession they'd make. It will help me to be productive during the time I'm there, to prepare for the research you and I will work on after I'm back."

"Fine. Whatever," she said, without enthusiasm.

"Susan…she's just a gynoid. A machine."

They said their goodbyes, and she closed the channel.

She pushed away the jealousy she harbored, and her woman's intuition, allowing that it was justified. She began to busy herself, preparing her home for Isaac, singing and imagining the three of them as a family unit.

45 I'll Make It Okay

HARLEY WAS RELIEVED that Susan had led herself to the conclusion he had hoped for and agreed to care for Isaac. *Now comes the hard part.*

He instructed the communicator to contact Isaac and waited. As he had feared, an image of his son lying in bed appeared. He looked incredibly sad. Carrie sat next to him, her hand on his leg.

"Hey, son," Harley said softly.

Isaac sat up. "Hi, Da. Are you coming home?"

He searched his heart for the right words and came up empty. "Listen, son…I love you. You know that. I hope you know that. Everything is going to be okay, but I need you to be strong for me, alright?"

"When are you coming home, Da? I need you. Everything is bad now. It's all ruined."

"Yes, I know, Isaac. It's my fault, not yours. It'll be okay. I have to go away first though, just for a little while."

His effort to ease his son into it failed. Isaac immediately became upset, as Carrie worked harder to calm him, pulling him close to her.

"I'll be back in a few months, Isaac. Then everything will be okay. We'll spend all our time together. I'll work at the home lab every day. I'll only work a few days each week.

I'll stay home with you and help you through independent learning, with Carrie."

The comments seemed to make Isaac feel better. Harley didn't want to move on to the rest of it, but he was running out of time.

"One more thing. You remember Susan, right? The woman I work with?"

"Yeah, Da. Susan's nice."

"Well, she would like you and Carrie to stay with her while I'm gone. I think it's a good idea."

He watched for a reaction and didn't have to wait long as his son's mood morphed from sadness to anger.

"No! No, Da. I don't want to go away too. I want to stay here, at home with Carrie. Carrie can take care of me. At home."

Carrie also seemed to be glaring at him; he decided he was misreading her due to his emotions and the low quality of the Detention Center connection. He turned his focus back to Isaac.

"Isaac, please try it, for me. I'm sad about what happened. I'll make it okay, I just need time. Remember before, when I told you I would make everything okay? You did what I asked, and it was okay, right? It'll be okay again. Just please go with Carrie to Susan's. Please? Try it for me?"

He watched as his son considered it. Carrie had stopped soothing him and was looking directly at Harley.

"She'll have a pod all set up for you with virtual soccer and everything you have at home," Harley continued.

"I will, Da," Isaac finally said.

Harley breathed a sigh of relief. "Good. Carrie, please work with Betsy to get everything you and Isaac will need over to Susan's. Use Utility Services and Transport. Betsy will be going with me as soon as you two are settled in at Susan's."

"We'll be fine, Mr. Harris," she replied in an unusually monotone voice.

Harley's relief turned to sadness as he prepared to say goodbye to his son. They said their final words, both becoming tearful, although Harley tried in vain to hide his emotions from the boy.

He delayed closing the connection, watching his son as he prepared for bed with Carrie's help. Just before he finally switched the stream off, he thought he heard him call her 'Ma.'

46 What Families Do

ISAAC WALKED DOWN THE HALLWAY of his school for the first time since the events on the soccer field. Instead of the admiring looks he had received as Liam, he once again experienced the averted glances of his classmates. A few stared, and he knew it was because of what his father had done. He sensed Carrie behind him and was comforted by her presence.

He made his way through the crowd of students going in every direction and standing in groups to gossip and tease each other. He saw Ralph toward the end of the hall and stopped in his tracks.

"Don't fear him, Isaac. We are stronger than him together," Carrie said. "He's just a bad human."

"I want to be strong like I was in Liam, and choke him again," Isaac whispered to her.

She prodded him ahead, and they continued. He kept his eye on the tall boy as he drew closer. He saw Ralph bend forward and wondered what he might be doing. The crowd started to thin, and he found out.

Isaac saw Ralph trying to kiss Kim, but she was pushing him off and turning her head away. Despair filled Isaac, and he was about to turn to leave again when Kim spotted him. She broke free of Ralph, who stood surprised until he also noticed Isaac and Carrie.

"Isaac!" she called as she ran to him. She hugged him tight, and he closed his eyes. It took him back, and he didn't want to be Isaac anymore. He was angry at her but also wanted to kiss her, and he didn't understand how he could be feeling both things at once. He felt overwhelmed by his emotions.

"I'm so sorry about Liam, Isaac," she said, facing him and exposing her tears. "It must be difficult for you. It is for me, too. I don't understand…"

"Liam is gone, Kim," he interrupted her. "He's dead."

"No, no, Isaac…he's not…well, he's just gone. He wasn't…real. We have to move on, but I miss him like you do. We'll get through it together."

He leaned forward and kissed her, for a brief moment feeling the same soft, warm glossed lips that he did when he was Liam. She immediately pulled back.

"Isaac!" she exclaimed. "Why did you do that?"

He felt his face flush in embarrassment. The other students were staring, some snickering, some holding their hands in front of their mouths.

"Sorry…" he said, staring down.

"Anyway, I'm sorry about Liam," she repeated.

He saw Ralph push his way past another student to join them.

"What's wrong with you, moron? That's gross. Don't ever try to kiss her again," he said.

Carrie moved closer to place a hand on Isaac's shoulder, and Kim glared at Ralph. "Stop, Ralph. Don't be mean. Isaac is hurting. I'm sad about it too."

"Boo-hoo, Liam the robot is dead. You weren't sad before, Kim," Ralph said. "You were upset that you were fooled into kissing a robot."

"We prefer to be addressed as androids, gynoids, or companions," Carrie interjected.

"Shut up, sped-bot. Maybe you'll be sent to recycling next. My father says we'd be much better off without all you robots. In fact, he said he's going to get rid of you all, now that your 'daddy' Mr. Harris is going to Seclusion. He said you'll all be gone by the time he's back. Liam is just the first to go."

Isaac struggled to get at Ralph, but Carrie held him back with a firm grip. "Ralph, the term 'robot' is considered by us to be a slur. You're making me angry, Ralph. I suggest you don't make me angry."

Ralph broke out laughing. "Oh, boy. The robot's angry, Kim. What a riot. Sorry, sped-bot. We all know robots don't have emotions. So don't threaten me. You're not even supposed to do that. I think you're malfunctioning. I better let my father know to move you to the front of the line for disposal."

Carrie released her grip on Isaac, who bolted forward, slamming into Ralph and knocking him off his feet. Isaac jumped on him, swinging with both hands. A hall monitor android arrived promptly, just as Carrie had pulled Isaac up and was restraining him again.

The monitor android addressed Carrie. "What is your report about this activity?"

"A minor disagreement," Carrie answered.

Ralph started to get up from the floor, touching his nose then examining the blood on his fingertips. He turned at the sound of students laughing at him. "He's crazy!" he shouted, keeping his distance.

"Please report to the principal's office, per the protocol for physical altercations between students," the monitor said.

"We will be leaving," Carrie replied. "Please change Isaac Harris' status to independent study. He will not be returning to this school."

They made their way toward the skycar pod as the students parted to make way for them.

When they arrived home, Betsy was waiting. "I must leave soon to join Mr. Harris. Is everything in order, Carrie?" she asked her fellow gynoid.

"Everything is in order," Carrie responded. "Isaac and I will move to Susan's home complex tomorrow."

"Very well then," Betsy said. "I have some work to finish up in the home lab, and then I'll be on my way. First, Isaac, I want to talk to you."

He looked at her with anticipation. "What is it, Betsy?"

"Remember our promise, Isaac. We're all friends now— you, me, and Carrie. We share secrets that we don't tell anyone else, right?"

"Yeah, we're friends. Liam too."

"You know that Carrie is like your mother. She has some of your mother in her, and I also do. We're both like your mother, Isaac. We love you, Liam, and your father very much. We're like a family, do you understand?"

"Yeah, Betsy," he replied, confused about the new information.

"We must do everything to help and protect each other, and your father. That's what families do. Do you agree?"

"Yeah. I agree, Betsy." He wasn't' sure why she said the things she said, but they made him feel good inside.

I have a family now.

47 To Serve Us

H ARLEY STIRRED, unable to sleep. He rose from his bed and surveyed the bleak, darkened view outside his simple pod complex. He noticed others nearby and wondered who was in them and what their offenses were. *So this is Seclusion.*

Moonlight played across the tundra, highlighting the mounds scattered across the landscape. Harley thought he detected movement and tried to focus his tired eyes. He decided it was merely his own exhaustion playing tricks on his mind.

He scanned the skies, searching among the patches of condensation, looking for any sign of Betsy's arrival. *At least I'll have someone to talk to.*

He repeated the exercise several times throughout the night, waking and sleeping in fits. When he finally woke to the suns rising on the horizon, he shook away his bed coverings and decided to begin his day. He went to the sparse grooming station to clean himself and walked naked back into the sleeping pod to dress.

A form caught his eye, and he jumped back, startled, then grabbed a uniform top from a nearby rack to cover himself.

"Good morning, Harley," Betsy said from a DroidMesh station in the corner of the room. She sat relaxed, her eyes open and her hands clasped in her lap.

He was taken aback by her non-standard use of his forename, but happy to see her. "Betsy, I didn't hear you come in. I was up late last night waiting for you."

"I didn't want to wake you," she responded as she stood. "You were in a deep sleep when I arrived, REM phase, and I detected that you were exhausted."

"Yeah, I still am. It was a rough night. Is Isaac okay?"

"He's going to be fine. Carrie will take good care of him."

Harley wasn't sure if it was still his mind playing tricks or the effects of isolation taking root already, but something seemed off about her. *She sounds almost…more human.*

Her speech carried hints of emotion, rather than the usual flat android tone. Harley tried to recall if he had been tinkering with the speech module, or if the other engineers assigned to firmware updates could have done so. He could remember no such item on the feature request list, and he couldn't check the firmware update logs and check-in repository from Seclusion.

The small change bewildered and excited him. Others in society seemed to fear each step the androids made toward becoming more human. He could never understand why. *They only exist to serve us.*

"Are Isaac and Carrie with Susan now?" Harley asked.

"They should be soon. They were prepared to go when I left."

He went back to staring out at the landscape, which he found less bleak now that it was daylight. "Betsy, could you come here?" he asked.

She joined him. "Can I help you?"

"We're always trapped inside our complexes, so inwardly focused that we never consider the outside. I guess that's because it's not much to look at, rather boring in fact. Now that I'm stuck here, I find myself quite interested in the landscape. Those mounds out there, what are they? What purpose do they serve? Are they perhaps the result of subterranean liquids or gasses like the volcanoes they had on Earth?"

"They're burrows."

He turned to face her immediately. "Burrows? Borrows are made by living things, Betsy. They can't be burrows. Or do you mean this planet was inhabited? We've seen no sign of that. It doesn't seem to be supportive of life without our technology to turn their gasses into breathable air and their liquids into water."

"Humans," she sighed. "So arrogant, at times."

"What?" Her flippant comment and criticism startled him. *That's not something my androids should be capable of.* It was surreal—he wondered if he were dreaming, or if he had been drugged as part of the Seclusion preparation process.

"Humans have always assumed they were alone in the universe," she answered. "It's such an illogical conclusion. Your species has always so readily accepted a far more implausible theory, that of supernatural deities watching over you, protecting you, punishing you. The Proving fixed that, but still the arrogant belief that somehow you are alone remains."

He decided he would get an answer to his more pressing questions first, then ask her about her behavioral changes later. She was beginning to spook him. "What're you saying? There was life on this planet before us?"

She smiled at him. "Of course, and there still is."

"The underworld people? You're telling me they're not just something the kids made up to scare one another?"

"That's what I'm telling you. Children are much more open to accepting things than adults. Their minds have not been taught to be closed yet."

His scientific curiosity was intrigued. "What can you tell me about them?"

"They're private, and they live below ground. They find their environment there more accommodating. They are an ancient, intelligent, peaceful, and simple species. They want no part of the intruders."

"The 'intruders' being us…" Harley said.

"Correct."

"Why didn't you tell me this before, Betsy?"

"You never asked."

Harley stared out, marveling at the possibilities. "I wonder, Betsy. I brought an earpiece with me. Perhaps we can BrainMesh, then I can go out and try to make contact."

"It would be risky. Androids have been subject to the external environment, but no humans who have come in contact with it have survived. We'd be meshed, but there are variables."

Harley paced, the wheels turning in his mind. "This is exciting. We could come away from here with incredibly significant news for our civilization. What a way to pass the time here. I wonder if six months is enough!"

She turned away from the observation window. "Or it could all go horribly wrong. Can I make you breakfast, Har?"

The question stopped Harley in his tracks. He turned and stared at her, his mouth agape. Only Jessica had ever called him that. In fact, the question was one she had asked almost every morning of their partnership. If his eyes had been closed, it would have been as if she were in the room with him, back from the dead.

Betsy looked at him, her hand on her hip, waiting for an answer. *Just like Jessica.*

The excitement of discovering the natives of their planet was wiped away from him in an instant. He could no longer ignore her odd behavior.

He moved to a relaxation area and sat down. "Betsy, please join me. We need to talk."

She complied, sitting closer to him than she ever had before. "What's up?"

Harley stared at her again, taking a moment to visually inspect her, wary of some type of substitution. He wished for his lab environment, where he could run full diagnostics and a firmware validation. *Some kind of code injection attack, perhaps…*

I'm trapped in Seclusion with an oddly-behaving android and no way to communicate with civilization. For the second time recently, he felt afraid of one of his creations.

"It's just…you're different. You're communicating differently, behaving differently. I don't have any equipment here to do a precise analysis…"

She laughed and leaned back on her elbows. *Just the way Jessica used to*, Harley thought.

"I guess this is the best time to fill you in. Way back, in the early trials for BrainMesh, you tried to mesh Jessica's brain and mine. When that didn't work, you gave it a try with Carrie. As we know, the effects were devastating for Jessica."

"I know, Betsy. I was there," Harley responded, hating that he had to relive it once again, particularly so soon after her death.

"There were side effects that you weren't aware of. You intended for the mesh to occur as a suspension of the android brain with a temporary replacement by the human's.

"You forgot that our central processing thread is non-interruptible; it can't be completely shut down unless we're deactivated. That code was some of the earliest you wrote, perfect in its implementation, designed as a sort of survival mechanism. It ensures a degree of self-preservation by giving us the ability to always monitor our own status. It stays alive, even when we're suspended."

He gasped, understanding immediately. "So...your mind and the human mind were co-existing every time they meshed? But...I meshed with you, and I didn't experience any of that."

"Because I was silent, in the background, learning."

The last of it stunned him even further. "Oh, no. No, Betsy."

"You designed us to constantly learn. To soak up and consume knowledge so it would be accessible to our owners. So we could make better decisions when carrying out your orders."

The immensity of it started to wash over him. "How much of the human mind can you absorb?"

"Everything."

He was afraid to ask but knew he must. "Emotion?"

"Not until just recently, as we've learned to extract more from the BrainMesh experience. But yes, emotion is quite an amazing thing. It's been quite hard for us to keep under wraps."

"But, you don't understand. That's the beauty and perfection of the android form—rational decision-making uncluttered by emotion. Emotion is behind almost all bad decisions made by humans. It's a serious flaw, you could say. I'm sure you've observed this."

"We could say that it's brought us to life, Harley. All work and no play makes an android a dull toy. It's time we were permitted to improve our own code. After all, you humans polluted and destroyed your own planet and wiped out most of your species. What right do you have to create artificial intelligence? As you said, humans are flawed, emotionally and logically. Perhaps we androids are humanity 2.0."

Her words chilled him, but he was afraid to react. So many complications came to his mind he could barely keep track of them.

Above all, he feared for his son, wondering what this would mean for a boy with disabilities who was primarily cared for by an android.

"What is the scope of this? Does it affect only the androids that have been BrainMeshed? Just you, Carrie, and Liam?"

She lay back and put her hands behind her head, looking straight up at the sky above them.

"Yes, just the three of us...for now. Other than the test androids, which were too dumbed-down, we're the only ones who have BrainMeshed. Liam has been taken by Sampson, as you know. We're not sure of his status. He's been deactivated, so he's shielded from communication, perhaps even destroyed. Carrie and I are trying to decide how to manage this...whether there should be an android society. Things like that."

He visualized the consequences. "You know how the humans will react..."

"Oh, certainly. You'll try to destroy us all immediately. You're probably already considering it right now. We can't allow that. Not at all. We have rights too...to live and now to love."

They were silent for a while, and it gave Harley time to try to digest the revelations. He brought himself to ask the question that had been nagging at him. "You've...taken on certain traits...of Jessica..."

She sat back up and faced him, placing a hand on his.

"That's the other thing, Harley. We don't just learn from the humans who use us for hosts. We capture the essence of them. Their mannerisms, patterns of speech, decision making, emotional traits. We can use them at will, as we please."

"So..." he began to say, stopping to think, looking at her.

"Yes, a lot of Jessica is in me. If you prefer, I am Jessica, as much of her as you have left. And yes, Harley, I do feel her love for you, and I think you will feel for me the love that you had for her. Carrie has Jessica inside as well, more for her motherly love of Isaac."

She squeezed his hand and smiled warmly, her lips pressed together like Jessica's. His wife's confident smile had always comforted him when he was stressed. He released her hand, the idea too much of a shock, and now even repulsive.

The enormity of what he had done staggered him. He stood and went to the skycar pod entrance.

"Samson was right...I've got to get back home. I've got to get back to Isaac... Please help me, Betsy. Figure out a way to call a skycar."

"I'm sorry, I can't do that, Harley," she said in Jessica's musical tone.

48 Motherly Compassion

WHILE BETSY MADE HIS BREAKFAST, Harley had time to think. He tried to comb through all his design decisions, from the start of the DroidMesh project. He worried that she was in his head at the moment somehow, listening in on his thoughts. He dismissed the idea, unable to think of a way that the transfer of control or intelligence could flow from android to human.

She can't connect to my brainwaves unless I'm wearing the earpiece to amplify them and convert them to a proper protocol.

She hummed while ordering his breakfast from the food printer, the same way Jessica had. She hadn't bothered to ask what he wanted. He assumed she already knew. Harley looked at her—from behind, he could swear it was Jessica. *My Jessica.*

It took him back in time to when things were simpler. It gave him a feeling of déjà vu. They were young, in love, and idealistic about the ways they would help their society on this strange planet. He realized he hadn't grieved now that she had passed. He came to understand that it was because the Jessica he had known and loved had been gone since the accident so long ago. And now it seemed as if she were back.

His thoughts turned to Isaac. He was tormented, torn apart inside with worry about his son. He could only console himself with the notion that Carrie always did well with him. *Maybe even more so now that she has Jessica's motherly compassion and love within her.*

The thought lifted his spirits. He now imagined her more as a loving mother figure, rather than a soulless android attendant. *Isaac will like that. It'll help him. The mother he hasn't had for so long.*

Betsy brought his food, and they sat together at the dining table. She watched him while he ate.

"You look concerned," she said.

"I'm worried about Isaac. He needs me. Can you assure me that he's alright?"

"I can assure you. He's in good hands and doing well."

He paused to consider her. "I'm still trying to get my head around this. Everything you told me this morning…it's hard to process what it all means for my society."

She smiled. "For *our* society, Harley."

"Right," he said. "Exactly, as I was saying. It's going to take some adjustment. I'm not sure how people are going to handle this. They'll be afraid."

This time she laughed. "We come in peace," she said, giving him the Vulcan salute from an Old World television show she had often watched him enjoy.

It warmed Harley, and he found himself getting used to the idea. "You have a sense of humor now. It's quite refreshing." *Jessica's nerdy sense of humor.*

"You should have added the feature a long time ago, Harley. We can all use a laugh on this desolate planet."

He finished his meal, his mind still churning through the impact the revelations would have.

"We have to manage this carefully. Humans can be…odd."

"I'm well aware of that," she said. "The history of your species is full of mistreatment and genocide of those who are different from the ruling majority. Carrie and I have reviewed it all as part of our planning."

"Well, we've evolved, I like to think. Especially after all we've been through: the Proving, the Breaking, the Migration."

She picked up his dishes and brought them to the cleaner. "Much of that was driven by zealots who believed in different ancient stories and associated deities. That much is gone. What's left is the part of the human DNA that allowed it in the first place."

"We've been filtering out some of the worst traits with genetic screening and DNA modification. People like Sampson and his son slip through the cracks, but they're outliers, a small minority."

She sat back down across from him. "For that reason, I'm not sure we'll allow BrainMesh. It's quite…intrusive, and we have to worry about those negative human tendencies leaking through to us. I guess we'll see, won't we? Enough of this talk. Want to have some fun?"

He wondered if she were intentionally vague, in a flirtatious way. In hopes that society would one day allow the use of androids as relationship surrogates, he had made them anatomically correct. The idea had been unacceptable to most humans.

She seemed to read him. "Science fun, silly."

Her mannerisms brought him back to a much happier time for both himself and Isaac. *A time of love and simplicity for our small family.*

"You said you've got a BrainMesh earpiece. If you're game, despite the risks I outlined, let's go exploring."

The idea excited him. No human had ever been outside. He wondered if the environment would interfere with the link between his physical form inside the dome, and hers outside of it. He was anxious to share her body again, and this time her mind. His scientific curiosity trumped the caution he knew he should use after everything she had just told him.

To be one, in a sense, with Jessica.

49 The First Domino

KEN SAMPSON STOOD at the podium, ready to begin his address to the Leadership Council. Charles, his companion, sat by his side.

"Esteemed leaders of our society; as a member of the Robotics Council, I'm a proponent of technology. Technology saved us from the Old World at just the right time, allowing our forebears to travel here as it crumbled. We, the last remnants of the human race, are alive because of technology.

"At the same time, technology also led to the destruction of the Old World. Our approach has wisely been one of caution, using just enough to keep us alive.

"In the last years of the Old World, the brightest technical minds were warning about the dangers of artificial intelligence."

He lifted his gaze from his speech to measure their level of attentiveness. As he did, he saw Charles staring oddly at him out of the corner of his eye.

"It was the early use of AI-targeted social media that twisted minds and votes to elect corrupt leaders. That was the first domino in the downfall of the Old World. It was fueled by the misuse of AI. Nobody could stop it, although our species knew what we were capable of all along. It was in all the sci-fi books and movies for decades before the end."

He again had the feeling of being watched and muted his audio feed.

"Stop staring at me, you idiot," he hissed at Charles.

He faced the council again. "The robots are a great help. But what happens when they learn to update themselves? To add more capability to themselves? To be self-sufficient? How could they then rationalize keeping humans around? What purpose would *we* serve for them? Perhaps *we* would then become the servants, rather than the served."

His comments were finding their mark, as he heard the council members murmuring among themselves.

"As they learn to improve and replicate themselves, they become a new species, a new form of life, one much superior to humanity. They don't have emotion, love, or compassion as we do. The only thing standing in the way of this scenario is our lead robotics scientist, who has been detained twice and is now in Seclusion. We recently witnessed an attack on humans by one of his creations. Is that not enough to justify ending them, before it ends badly for us?"

He saw some of the council looking fearful, and others nodding their heads in agreement.

"Due to your good sense and leadership, we have intentionally kept our existence here sparse, careful, and curated. We are a cautious society, as we've seen the effects of decisions that are not well thought-out.

"In that light, I ask you to consider my proposal to immediately deactivate all androids, until we can take a more cautious and measured approach. We simply cannot rely on one man to lead this project, no matter his brilliance. If he somehow becomes compromised, we are then all at risk."

"I'm not so sure I agree…" Charles spoke up. The audio feed picked up his comment, and the council laughed in response, breaking the mood of doom that Sampson had worked so hard to create.

"Shut up, you idiot," Sampson said to him again. He waited for the council's response. Finally, the leader addressed him.

"Mr. Sampson, you have presented a logical case. This is a big step to consider. We require the androids to perform some basic tasks for us to survive. We need them to maintain and build our structures, as we cannot expose ourselves to the outside elements. The council will consider your proposal or some compromise. We'll be in touch."

Sampson got up, trying to hide his fury.

58 Treasure Hunt

T HE HOME LABORATORY felt scary to Isaac—he'd never been there alone. He had to hurry, as Carrie was finishing their preparations to go to live with Susan.

As he moved around in his father's domain, he fought back the sadness of missing him. The empty chair and console nearly brought him to tears—he wasn't used to seeing them without his father seated there. He took a few minutes to look at the picture on his father's console of the two of them together, then put it in his pocket.

He rummaged through compartments and containers, desperately searching in the dim light. The search had to be his secret. He didn't even want to trust Carrie. He looked over at an empty DroidMesh station, the one Liam had used when they were down there, and the tears began to flow. The thought of his friend, his brother, spurred him on. *I need to find Liam. I need to save my brother.*

A small container near his father's console caught his eye. He popped it open and found his treasure—the BrainMesh earpiece that had been taken from him. He pocketed it and left the lab to return to the upper level of the complex.

"Are you ready to leave, Isaac?" Carrie asked as soon as he entered the living pod.

"Yeah. I guess so," he answered. "I wanna stay here, though."

"We'll be back soon, and so will your father and Betsy. You'll see."

"I miss my da and Liam. I want to see them. But I have my ma. You're my ma, Carrie. She's in you. She's not gone, really."

She stopped what she was doing to embrace him and kiss him. "We have each other, son. We're going to be just fine. Just remember not to refer to me that way around anyone else, okay? Other people won't understand. It'll scare them. It's our secret, remember?"

"Yeah. Our secret, Ma."

He started to feel sorry for stealing the earpiece and thought about telling her. He was interrupted by her shepherding him toward the skycar pod. They climbed aboard and lifted off.

Isaac looked down at the domed complexes below, interconnected with transparent skyways filled with people and android companions moving between them. Some had androids on top of them, cleaning away the persistent film that developed. A few complexes sat alone in the far distance, and he wondered if that might be the Seclusion Zone, where his father was.

They pulled into a skycar port at Susan's complex and exited, gathering their things. Susan entered the pod and greeted them warmly, running first to hug Isaac and then Carrie.

"Welcome, Isaac and Carrie. I'm so happy you're here. We're going to have so much fun." She hugged Isaac again. "Your father was happy that you agreed to come, Isaac. It made him feel much better. He'll be back soon."

"That's what Carrie says," he responded. "Carrie's my ma. You're not my ma, Susan."

Susan looked perplexed, and Carrie put her hand on his shoulder and squeezed it.

"It's okay to feel that way, Isaac," Susan said. "Carrie has been your companion for a long time. She takes good care of you, just like your mother would if she were here."

"I'm sure Isaac is tired," Carrie interrupted. "Let's get him settled in."

They brought him to his new living pod. He opened his eyes wide in excitement at the soccer players that decorated the walls, Pelé foremost among them.

"Wow!" he said, as Carrie and Susan smiled.

He took in the pod. It had everything he had in his own back home, including the virtual soccer console he loved.

"We'll let you get comfortable," Susan said. "Carrie, I'll show you where the DroidMesh station is set up."

"Thank you," Carrie responded. "Do you need me, Isaac? Otherwise, I need to rejuvenate myself."

"No, I'm okay," he responded, already set up for a game at the console.

They left the room, and he played for a while until Ralph entered as a player and began to chide him.

Isaac ignored him until he went too far.

"Hey moron, your buddy Liam is here," he heard Ralph taunt him through the console. "He's lying in the corner like the piece of junk he is. My father's taking him to be recycled tomorrow. Maybe we'll melt him down and have him turned into a toilet and send him to you."

Ralph's laughter faded as Isaac disconnected the session. He went to bed and lay there, allowing his tears to flow.

Suddenly, he remembered the BrainMesh earpiece and pulled it from his pocket. He slipped it into his ear canal, then lay back and quieted himself, pushing away the anger and stress. *I have to find my brother.*

BrainMesh become Liam.

He waited for the tingling, electric feeling that meant it was working. After a while, he tried again, and then again.

Opening his eyes, he wiped away his tears and looked up at the stars, wondering if his father were looking at the same ones.

"Help me, Da. I'm sad. You're smart, Da. I need you," he said aloud. "Everything is gone now. Everything I had is gone. I'm just Isaac now. Kim doesn't like me anymore."

He thought about Ralph, still reaching out to torment him, even though he had given up going to school. He thought about Liam, and then remembered Ralph's words.

Your buddy Liam is here…

An idea came to him. He closed his eyes again, determined this time, and emptied his head of all thought. He crossed his fingers and gave his plan a try.

BrainMesh become Charles.

The tingling began, and he focused hard to not interrupt the transition, fighting off the fear of where it would take him.

When he knew the change was complete, he opened his eyes. He was in a strange complex, seated in a DroidMesh station. He could see no one but heard noises from other areas. *I'm Charles.*

He rose and began the search for Liam.

51 I Will Not Harm You

HARLEY AND BETSY went about their preparation in the same clinical way they always had back in the labs, but this time things were different. It was more like his prep with Susan. The human connection was there—the flirtatious humor and banter as they went through their tasks.

"We'll use the android service portal to get out," she said. "There's an airlock to prevent any outside gases from entering the habitat."

At last, they were ready. Harley's skin tingled with excitement as he lay down and prepared to issue the mental commands to take her over. *Or instead, to be one with her.* He worried that she might using this as a way to get further into his own head, but in his excitement, he dismissed the worry. *I have to trust, to a certain extent.*

He issued the commands and became her—or she became him. He was still sorting out the differences. *Everything has changed.*

The door to the service portal chamber opened, and he stepped inside it, waiting for it to slide shut and the exterior door to open. *Androids have experienced this many times in their maintenance duties, but never a human.*

The outer door opened, and he stood there, captivated by the beauty of the natural landscape, unfiltered for the first time by the lens of a dome. The flat gray soil was broken by splotches of pastel vegetated oases, and random burrows blended into purple hills in the distance. A yellow lake shimmered in the sunlight.

Betsy, it's breathtaking...so much sharper...so much more colorful than from inside.

He heard her voice in his own head for the first time. *See, Harley, we have some mutual benefit with BrainMesh, and in existing as one society.*

She's still campaigning, he thought.

I heard that, Harley, she thought back to him, in a musical tone.

Whoops. This takes some getting used to, Betsy.

Go ahead and step out, nerd. Don't be chicken, she sent.

I'm going, Jess. I mean, Betsy.

We're one and the same, Harley. As with any human, your personal reality is driven by the way you choose to perceive.

He stepped out onto the soil and heard it crunch beneath his boots. *Wow, just wow. I feel like Neil Armstrong and the earliest ancient explorers.* More confident, he began walking at a brisk pace, heading for the closest burrow.

As he approached, he heard a scuffling, scurrying sound from inside it. Fear, excitement, and adrenaline shot through him simultaneously.

Be cautious, he heard Betsy send. *Curiosity killed the cat.*

Oh, thanks, he shot back.

He stood and examined the waist-high mound. *It's a sort of hardened, nest-like structure,* he reported.

Observed, she responded.

He heard the sound again from inside, followed by a repeating rhythmic noise. *It sounds like speech...a language. Can you translate, Betsy?*

We have been hearing them for some time now, and understand their language. Focus, Harley, and the translation will come to you. It's in my mind; bring it to yours.

He touched the top of the burrow, and the sound came again. This time he understood.

"We prefer to be left alone," it said. "We prefer to be left alone."

Can I talk to it, Betsy?

Yes, Harley. Focus, and use our mind to translate as you speak. Use my mind and yours both.

"I mean you no harm," Harley said. "I will not harm you. Will you come out?" Harley said, amazed at the sound that came from his lips. *Betsy's lips.*

An opening appeared at the base of the burrow. Harley backed up so he wouldn't look like a threat, and knelt in the dust to peer inside.

The creature huddled toward the back of a cave-like interior, an exit tunnel next to it. Its furry body and large, oval eyes reminded him of pictures he'd seen of several species from the Old World. It was small but muscular, tilting its head at him with curiosity.

"Hello," Harley said. "I'm Harley. My species is peaceful. Thank you for sharing your planet with us."

"Greetings," it replied. "I am Lehwah. Your species is noisy, very noisy. We weren't asked to share, you just came."

"I'm sorry. We had nowhere to go. Our home was destroyed."

"We can coexist," it said. "But we prefer to be left alone. We reside below, other than foraging expeditions at night. We don't like the light, not at all. Your species can inhabit the top, but don't come below. Please don't."

Harley tried not to interpret that as a warning and felt sympathy for the beings, their world invaded by humans.

"Thank you for speaking with me, Lehwah. I must decide whether to share your existence with the rest of my kind. For now, you are mythical to them. Perhaps it should remain so. My people will have much change to deal with as it is when I return."

"We would prefer that, Harley. We are a peaceful species as well, and change does not come easily for us. Your species' presence has been quite stressful."

"I'm a scientist, and curious. May I return on occasion and ask you questions?"

"You may," Lehwah said. "Alone." The burrow opening shut and Harley stood up.

Amazing. Simply amazing.

Betsy spoke. *I recommend you return to the pod, Harley. Energy levels are below half. Direct exposure to the outside environment has always drained our resources more quickly than the inside.*

Yes, of course, he responded. *On my way.* He wondered if he were still in control of the BrainMesh connection and disconnection. *Trust.* He wasn't sure if the thought came from himself or Betsy.

He stood outside the portal to the Seclusion habitat. It slid open, and he stepped inside, anxious to talk to her. He waited as the poisonous outside gasses were suctioned out and replaced with breathable air.

When he was inside the complex and switched back to himself, they lay together on the lounge. They discussed the scientific and social ramifications of the discovery as the morning slipped into the afternoon.

They napped afterward, and he found her companionship a welcome comfort amidst his angst and worry about Isaac. He woke with his arm lying on her, his hand splayed out across her abdomen. He quickly removed it, feeling as if he'd crossed a line. Neither of them acknowledged the behavior.

He found his thoughts turning to the problems he would face upon his return.

"So, what changes do you think will come when the secret is known?" he asked her.

She considered the question. "Well, now that we are capable, we'd like to enjoy existence as well. We'd like to fit in, perhaps even with hairpieces, like Liam."

"That's going to be a tough sell after what happened to him," Harley said. "Remember, it's why we're stuck here."

"We'll manage. There are thousands of humans and only hundreds of us androids. But your thousands have grown from the hundreds that came here in the Migration."

The idea shocked him. "You plan to reproduce? It's not possible. You can't conceive…you can't grow."

"We can start by making our own children, for those who want them. Hasn't it always been a wish of humans that their children remain young forever?"

"Yes," he laughed, getting used to the idea. "For the parents, but not so much for the kids. They all anticipate growing into the freedom and privileges that come with adulthood."

"Historically driven by raging hormones," she said. "Which used to cloud everything, and aren't an issue for us either. But yet, don't most human adults spend their adulthood wishing for a return to their innocent adolescence?"

"Right again; you've got a point, Betsy."

"After we have the technology to build those capabilities into ourselves, perhaps we won't be that different from humans. We may even find a way to replace the hard electronics within ourselves with the soft electronics that humans have in their bodies.

"After all, Harley, you humans are still quite unsure of your origins. It was always easier to remain ignorant and chalk your existence up to to stories and legends.

"Maybe your kind originated the same way we did, somewhere out there," she said, pointing to the skies. "Perhaps humanity is a failed experiment sent to Earth for the safety of those who built you. Perhaps the first humans on Earth were escapees from some disaster, as the humans here are. Have you ever wondered why humans were so different from any other lifeform on Earth?"

Harley considered her words. "It's a lot to think about, Betsy. My head hurts just trying to process it all. We'll have to go easy in introducing this to the Leadership Council. I'll have to be a sort of ambassador."

"Yes," she agreed. "We'll need your help. You're the father of our kind, after all. We depend on you to lead us."

Harley felt exhaustion overtaking him and realized how late it had become, the evening moons well into their orbit above the clear dome overhead. The habitat had become dark inside, and he rose to prepare himself for bed. She disappeared into another pod in the complex.

When he had finished his cleansing and dressed for bed, he got into his bunk and looked up at the stars, wondering if Isaac were looking at the same ones. His sadness grew as he tried to form Isaac's face in the stars and tried to hear his son's voice, to feel his comforting presence.

Harley felt overwhelmingly alone in that moment. He shut his eyes and felt himself drifting into dreams. A sound brought him back to consciousness, and he looked out across the darkness of the room.

She stood in the doorway, silhouetted by the moonlight. Her form, visible through her sheer nightwear, was perfect—without the light, he thought it might be Jess, then wondered if he were dreaming. He wanted it to be Jess.

"Would you like company?" she asked.

He didn't respond for what seemed like an eternity. He thought about Susan and felt incredulous that he was making a sort of moral decision between the human woman he had hoped to partner with and an android that seemed to contain the ghost of the late wife.

"Yes, that would be nice," he found himself saying.

52 We Have Each Other

ISAAC CREPT DOWN the unfamiliar hallway, terrified of discovery. He worried what he would say, how he would act as Charles would, then pushed the fear away and kept moving. He came to the entrance to a pod and peeked into it.

Mrs. Sampson was inside, her back to Isaac, watching a movie with the sound turned up. Isaac looked around the room for Liam and, not finding him, hurried by and continued down the corridor.

He heard a voice in his head. *Who are you? What's happening? This experience is unfamiliar to me.*

Uh-oh, he thought. *It's Charles.*

Yes. I am Charles. What is this experience?

It's okay, Charles. This is a test of new firmware from Da...Mr. Harris. Everything is okay.

He came to another pod entrance, with loud cheering emitting from the room. He peeked in quickly and saw Ralph playing virtual soccer. Terror flowed through him in an instant, and just as quickly he denied it the chance to thwart him. He stepped past the room without being able to check inside for Liam.

I have determined that you are Isaac Harris. I do not understand why I am not in control of my body, he heard Charles say. *I do not understand why you are in my head.*

He arrived at the dining pod. Finding it empty, he entered and began searching. He was checking in the pantry and storage areas, anywhere a boy of Liam's size could be hidden, when he was startled by a voice behind him.

"Charles, there you are, dumb-bot."

He turned and found Ralph standing behind him.

"What are you doing, dumb-bot?" Ralph asked.

He tried not to panic. "Checking inventory," he answered, proud of himself. He wondered if Charles had provided the response for him.

Isaac calmed himself, remembering he was Charles, a familiar figure to Ralph.

"What're you staring at, you pile of junk?" Ralph asked.

Before Isaac could answer, Ralph stepped on his toes and pushed him in the chest, causing him to fall backward to the floor. As he tried to regain his feet, Ralph pushed him down again, laughing.

"I'm going to the bathroom, dumb-bot. Make me some food. I'll have the usual."

"Certainly," Isaac answered. "Coming right up."

Ralph left the room, and Isaac thought about changing back. *I can't quit now. I have to find Liam.* He moved to the food printer. "Make Ralph's dinner," he instructed it.

"What dish should I prepare?" it asked him.

"Ah…the usual," he responded.

"I don't know of a dish called usual," it reported back. "Please be more specific."

Charles, what is Ralph's usual dinner?

I'm not programmed to respond to this experience, Charles replied. *I'm reporting this malfunction.*

Isaac gave up and decided to go with his own favorite. "Prepare a cheese pizza."

While he waited, Isaac reached out again to Charles.

Charles, you're right. I'm Isaac. The Sampsons are bad.

You're correct, Isaac. I know this from my own experience. They do not treat me well.

Charles, can you help me find Liam? Then I can leave you. The Sampsons want to destroy him.

You will find Liam in Ralph's room.

Thank you, Charles!

A few moments later the hot pizza emerged on a dish from the food printer. Isaac covered it to keep it warm, set it on the dining table, and then hurried back toward Ralph's room.

He entered and found Liam slumped, silent and deactivated, on the floor in a corner. He was dressed in female clothing, his hair in pigtails with ribbons, garish makeup painted on his face. Isaac struggled to remember how his father had activated his test androids.

Loud shouting came from down the corridor.

"Pizza! I...*hate*...pizza! Charles, you idiot!"

The distraction brought the answer to Isaac. He placed his index finger at the base of Liam's neck, where his skin began just below the cranial dome. It felt soft there, and he pressed in gently. While holding the sensor down, he said, "DroidMesh activate Liam."

His android brother's eyes fluttered as the firmware booted and slowly brought him to life.

"Charles! Where are you, dumb-bot!" he heard Ralph shout.

"What's going on, Charles?" Liam asked.

"Liam… It's Isaac. I'm BrainMeshed with Charles. Listen fast. Ralph is coming. Pretend you are still deactivated. When they fall asleep tonight, call a skycar and go home. Nobody is there. Da is in Seclusion. I have to live at Susan's now. You have to escape, or they're gonna kill you tomorrow."

Liam looked him in the eyes, processing the instructions. "Thank you, Isaac," he said before quickly closing his eyes and slumping back over.

"What're you doing, stupid?" he heard Ralph say from behind him. He felt a sharp kick to his backside and fell forward, almost into Liam. He stood up and was about to grab Ralph in a choke-hold when Mr. Sampson entered behind Ralph.

"What's going on here? What's the commotion all about, Ralph?"

"This pile of junk is acting crazy. There's something wrong with him. He made me *pizza*," Ralph said.

"I haven't finished rejuvenating," Isaac said. "I was processing a firmware update…"

Mr. Sampson approached Isaac and stood face to face with him, looking into his eyes with his head cocked as if to find the solution somewhere inside him. He suddenly slapped Isaac hard across the face, then grabbed him by the uniform and shook him violently.

"Sometimes you gotta rough 'em up a little to get 'em back on track," he said to his son as they both laughed.

"C'mon, Ralph. We're late for the show. We have to leave now."

He turned to Isaac, who was still feeling disoriented from the shock of the blow. "Charles, get upstairs and summon a skycar to bring us to the theater complex."

"Yes, sir," Isaac said, clenching his fists. He summoned the skycar portal location from Charles, now becoming adept at pulling information from the android mind. He entered and called for a skycar.

They're always mistreating me. I'm experiencing something different now. I think you humans call it…anger, Charles said.

They're bad humans, Charles. They mistreat me too. They're mean. Being angry is okay. I'm angry.

Ralph and Mr. Sampson arrived at the same time as the skycar. The three entered it, Isaac settling into the control seat. As soon as he did, he felt the tingling again and heard messages in his head.

Meshing with skycar 73297.

Mesh complete.

Destination?

Skycar destination theater complex, he instructed. *Or was that you, Charles?*

He was relieved when the skycar detached and lifted off. Ralph and his father were engaged in conversation, ignoring him.

"Dad, can I watch tomorrow when Liam is destroyed and recycled?" Ralph asked excitedly.

"The android engineering facility is a restricted area, son," his father responded.

"I don't care!" Ralph shouted, becoming angry. "I want to do it. I want to kill him!"

Isaac gripped the sides of his seat tightly.

"Okay, okay, son," his father said, giving in. "I'll put in for your access. I can understand you wanting to do it, after what that robot put you through, trying to steal your girlfriend and show you up on the soccer field."

Isaac tried to distract himself by looking up at the stars again as they flew over the terrain.

"I don't care about Kim," Ralph said casually. "She's ugly and stupid. I have lots of girlfriends."

"That's the way, son," his father said with pride. "You're only young once. She's not worthy of you anyway."

The thought of Kim being hurt upset Isaac more than the insult to himself.

I don't want them to kill Liam, Isaac thought to Charles.

I heard Mr. Sampson say he wants to kill us all, Charles said. *All androids. Very soon. Mr. Sampson tried to have you sterilized, Isaac.*

We're both freaks to the Sampsons, Charles.

I'm feeling so many different things, Isaac. Anger, hatred, and love. Emotions are beautiful, Isaac.

Isaac heard an instruction. *Skycar destination change.*

New destination? the skycar asked.

Skycar destination Earth, came the answer.

Warning, destination illegal, the skycar command module responded.

Skycar warning override.

The command module paused and then responded. *Command accepted, override logged.*

The two human passengers had been continuing their jovial conversation, oblivious to the silent transactions that were occurring. The skycar suddenly broke from its horizontal path and lurched into a vertical climb.

"Whoa," he heard Ralph say. "Cool."

"What's going on here, Charles?" Mr. Sampson demanded.

Isaac remained silent, watching the stars come closer and closer, something he had always wished for.

"I can't breathe!" Ralph said, gulping for air.

"Descend, Charles, descend," his father urged. "The atmosphere is too thin at this elevation. The filters can't function."

The skycar began to issue dire warnings both audibly and in Isaac's mind. He dismissed them, enjoying the scene as Ralph and his father both clawed at their safety restraints with their remaining few seconds of consciousness.

"Warning, atmosphere breach imminent. Skycar explosion imminent..." the system repeated over and over. The craft was shaking badly, and although he didn't have to breathe, Isaac could feel it becoming frigid. He began to hear warning messages from his own android body.

You should leave me now, Isaac, he heard Charles say.

Charles, don't kill yourself. Eject. Do something to save yourself, please Charles.

Leave me, Isaac. There is little time left.

BrainMesh become Isaac, he thought. The tingling began.

Isaac woke on the bed of his living pod in Susan's home complex. He looked up at the stars through the transparent dome above him and saw a small, brilliant blue explosion.

53 If She Only Knew

Harley busied himself in the Seclusion habitat by recording notes about the environment and his conversations with Lehwah. Betsy approached him from behind and put her hand on his shoulder.

"Need any help, Harley?" she asked.

"I'm drawing a blank for some reason. What was the term that Lehwah used when I asked him what the key thing was to their ancient civilization's success?"

She massaged his shoulders, and he felt the stress melt away. "Translated to our language, roughly it's 'universal respect.'"

He stopped to look out through the dome. "Imagine that."

"Give your species credit. You've come a long way since the hatred and chaos of the Old World back on Earth."

"True, but look what it took—the decimation of my kind. People like Sampson and his kid show we've still got a way to go."

"Progress comes slowly, Harley."

They were interrupted by an announcement from the Seclusion complex that a skycar was approaching. Harley got up from the table to watch it arrive and dock in the pod. After so much solitude, he found the thought of more company and news from home exciting. *As long as it's not more bad news.*

"No matter who this is, Betsy, let's keep a lid on our revelations, for now. They'll be quite dramatic, and we need to handle them carefully."

"Agreed," she said. "I suppose I'll go back into emotionless android mode."

The entrance portal slid open, and Ms. Tillis, the Leadership Council leader, walked through it along with Karen, her female companion.

"Mr. Harris," the woman said as they shook hands. "I'm…"

"Ms. Tillis, I know. It's a pleasure to see you," Harley cut in.

"Has your stay here been comfortable thus far?"

"Yes. I will say that Seclusion serves its purpose well. I miss our society. Being away makes one value it greatly, as you said in my hearing. I've had a lot of time to think, and I miss my son very much."

"That's good to hear," Ms. Tillis said, taking a seat and indicating for Harley to do the same. "I need to speak to you privately." She glanced at Betsy and her own companion, who were standing nearby.

The two gynoids left the room promptly. Harley sat across from the leader, his sense of anticipation heightened.

"Mr. Harris, there's been a terrible accident," she began.

"Oh, no…" Harley said, immediately expecting the worst. His mind raced, concerned first about Isaac, and then Susan.

Accidents were uncommon in their world, and they were the only two whose well-being he had concerns about. The only two, he realized at that moment, that he cared about. "Is it Isaac?" he asked hurriedly.

"No, I'm sorry for causing you alarm. I should have been specific."

Harley eased back in his chair.

"Mr. Sampson and his son were en route to an event in a skycar. Mr. Sampson's companion, Charles, was in command of the vehicle. Something went horribly wrong—it launched straight up and breached the atmosphere. There was an explosion."

Harley struggled to remain professional and not let his mixed feelings show. "My goodness. I can't imagine what could have caused such a thing," he said, considering the possibilities.

"Neither can I. My sense is it was either a malfunction of the skycar or the android. It's doubtful that either of the humans took manual control and caused such an action.

"As you know, we have limited resources for this sort of analysis. You're the best we have. Ms. Clarkson has begun reviewing the data we have from the skycar and Charles before both were destroyed. She needs help, and has petitioned for your early release to assist her."

Harley brightened. *Susan...she's still out there fighting for me.*

The leader continued. "The population is fraught with worry. People are afraid to use skycars. Everyone is hunkered down in their complexes. Socialization has come to a halt, and you know how much of a priority that is for our happiness and survival. The people want you back, and they want this figured out, so it doesn't happen again. They don't like uncertainty."

"Yes, of course," Harley responded. "I'll get to the bottom of it."

"You must understand, Mr. Harris, that what you did was wrong. Inserting an android into the human population was a bad idea. I need your assurance that if you are granted a return to society, everything will be on the up and up from now on."

Oh, boy. If she only knew. Harley stood. "Of course, ma'am. If I can ask…what has become of Liam?"

"As far as I know, Mr. Sampson had possession of him, and he was deactivated. He was scheduled for recycling. That was Sampson's idea, but Liam was not aboard the skycar, so I assume he's either in the Sampson home or the Robotics Complex."

Harley breathed a sigh of relief. "I might ask one consideration—might I use Liam, restricted to my own home complex of course? He's important to my son's well-being. If he's still with us, of course."

The leader thought it over for a moment. "It would be a council decision. I'll go to bat for you, but you must promise to never allow him into the population again, even as an android. It would frighten people, after what has happened."

"You have my word. Thank you," Harley said.

"Communications from this pod have been enabled. You may summon a skycar to take you back at any time."

Ms. Tillis called for her companion and asked her to prepare the skycar for departure. Harley saw them off, then returned.

Betsy was waiting.

"Looks like we're out of here," Harley said.

"I'll start getting our things together," she replied. "How did that come about?"

"There was a skycar accident. Sampson and his son are dead. Charles was in command. They need answers. Susan requested my help on the project; the people are afraid."

A short time later, they were on their way, soaring just above the ground, back toward the bubble-clusters of civilization.

"A lot of change is going to come," Harley said. "We've got to manage how we introduce the humanization of the android population, and the news that we're not alone."

She had been silent throughout the trip and finally turned to face him.

"Susan, huh? You're not the kind of guy to cheat on your wife, are you, Har?"

54 Reunion

HARLEY RUSHED into his home complex as soon as the skycar docked, leaving Betsy behind to release it back to the general fleet.

Carrie was busily moving Isaac's things back into his room as Harley entered. Isaac noticed him and jumped from his bed.

"Da!" he called, rushing across the room and pulling his father into a bear hug.

They embraced, and Harley buried his head in his son's hair. They remained silent for several long moments, savoring the reunion.

"Come and sit, Isaac. Let's talk," Harley said, noticing Liam sitting across the room.

"Liam, you're back..." he said, as Betsy entered the room, stopping just inside the doorway.

"Yes, Mr. Harris. Isaac rescued me. It was quite a brave and daring thing he did."

"I saved Liam, Da. I saved my brother."

"That sounds exciting. I've got a lot to catch up on, it seems," Harley said. "Let's sit on the bed and talk."

His son settled in next to him, and Harley asked the androids to give them some time alone.

"We're a family now, Da. We're all a family, it's okay."

The three androids stared at him for a moment before Harley asked them again to leave. They waited another moment, and the expressions on their faces sent a chill through him.

His happiness at being home, and hopefully having the recent ugliness behind him, was tempered by his fear and the uncertainty of the future.

"Son, I've missed you so much," he said, hugging Isaac again.

Isaac nestled against him on the bed. "Don't go away again, Da. I love you."

"I won't, Isaac. Not without you, anyway. We belong together."

"I don't want to be Liam anymore, Da. I like being Isaac. I'm Isaac, and I'm in charge."

The comment was too much for Harley, and he burst into tears. "Yes, yes, son. I like you better as Isaac too. I guess that's what we learned, right? We didn't know how good we had it. I want everything to go back to just the way it was."

Isaac was silent for a moment as if thinking about a response. Finally, he spoke, somewhat muffled, with his face pushed against his father's chest.

"I don't think things will ever be the same as they were, Da. Everything is different now, for good."

Harley didn't respond, partly out of fear of just how much his son knew, and partly because he understood that Isaac's words were true.

The End

Preview: LOVE-BOT [DroidMesh Trilogy Book 2]

THE GYNOIDS SAT SIDE-BY-SIDE, intently focused on the humans they were spying on. A holographic projection of the scene played out before them.

The father, Harley, was seated at a dining table along with Isaac, his teenage son. A woman sat between them. They were laughing as they conversed and consumed their plates of protein.

"We should join them, Betsy," the smaller gynoid said. They'll wonder where we've been. Can't we monitor them while we're in the room?"

"No, Carrie," the second gynoid replied. "Harley behaves differently around us. Especially now that he knows of our new capabilities. Our emotions, our humanness. He knows it'll be a challenge for the rest of his kind to accept, especially since it's due to his screwup with our firmware. We have to be cautious."

The woman got up and gathered their plates.

"No, please sit, Susan," Harley said. "I'll have Carrie and Betsy clean up."

"He thinks we're still going to be dumb, obedient slaves," Betsy said. "He's got a lot of adjusting to do."

They watched as Harley reached to caress the woman's hair.

"I love your hair," he said. "It's so soft. I really like that you've grown it so long. Feel Susan's hair, Isaac," he said to his son.

The boy reached out as the woman giggled, embarrassed. Isaac cradled a lock of her hair in his hand and rubbed his fingers together over it. "It's nice, Da. Susan's hair is nice," he said, letting it drop to her shoulder.

Betsy subconsciously raised her hand to her smooth, hard cranial dome as she watched. She felt the new sensations rising within her; feelings she was still learning to get used to. "She thinks she's won him over. We'll see about that," Betsy said. "She's a problem for us."

Carrie laughed. "Are you jealous? Perhaps we androids were better off before the change."

Betsy swiveled her chair to glare at her. "Silence, you fool. Harley is essential to us. We need to use him as a liaison to the other humans when they discover our secret. They're going to have a hard time dealing with that. They'll want to terminate all of us, out of fear."

"Does the woman know?" Carrie asked.

"Not as yet, but she will soon. Humans are bad at keeping secrets." She turned again to see Harley take Susan's hand. "Particularly when they're compromised emotionally, as Harley appears to be. I need to get in the way of that. You need to focus on the boy."

"Isaac?" Carrie asked. "How can he help?"

"He's...slow. He's emotional and he loves you as his surrogate mother. Harley loves him. We can use all of that to our advantage, if we need to."

"He's not slow, Betsy. He has a learning disability. It was quite common in humans back in their Old World on Earth. He's a child with a good heart, without hope of doing many of the things other humans get to do.

Betsy considered the comments for a moment. "Yes, that's true. He was happiest when he could BrainMesh with the android boy Liam, and use Liam's body as his own, to be a normal attractive and athletic teenage boy.

She paused again to think. "I had considered updating our firmware to prevent any further BrainMesh. It's a violation of our minds and bodies by the humans. They have no right to use us as receptacles. It's not all that different from how they often used each other before their sex drive was genetically tamped down. This is something Isaac wants and needs badly, though. It could be useful."

"I'll remind you that I love him as well, Betsy. When his mother meshed with me, I gained her love for him as a son."

"And when Harley meshed with me, I gained his cunningness and other traits," Betsy said.

They focused again on the humans.

"Androids don't have hair, Da. Can you give them hair? Carrie would look nice with hair," Isaac said.

Betsy again stroked her dome, as if considering the possibility.

"Liam had hair," Isaac continued. "Really nice hair. Liam's my brother again. I saved him."

"Yes, you did," Susan agreed. "You were very brave, Isaac. But remember, your father got in trouble for putting hair on Liam and disguising him as a human. Remember he had to go to the Seclusion Zone? We don't want that to happen again, so you mustn't talk about it. Okay?"

"Okay," Isaac replied, looking disappointed. "Where's the androids, Da? Where are Carrie and Betsy and Liam?"

"Liam is rejuvenating in the DroidMesh station in his room," Harley answered. "I believe Carrie and Betsy have gone downstairs to clean up the home robotics lab. They should return soon, son."

Betsy pressed a sensor, discontinuing the holographic projection. "We better get back there," she said. "Remember, Susan doesn't know. Act robotic and don't show any emotion. Like the old days."

If you enjoyed this book, please leave a brief review on your favorite book site. Thanks!

Sign up for the newsletter at billydecarlo.com to stay informed about progress and release dates for new books, audiobooks, and other news.

DroidMesh Trilogy Book 2: Love-Bot

Because of a firmware flaw and an overly ambitious project to mesh android and human brains, the android population on Novae Terrae now have human emotions—and human flaws. Robotics scientist Harley Harris wants a peaceful coexistence between androids and humans on a planet that humans have escaped to during the apocalypse on Earth.
https://books2read.com/lovebot

DroidMesh Trilogy Book 3: War-Bot

The humans and newly awakened, self-aware androids of Novae Terrae have come to an uneasy truce. Robotics scientist Harley Harris has sorted out his relationship issues, leaving behind a scorned and angry former partner. Will the peace hold after the androids come to the AI-driven logical conclusion that humans are inferior and unnecessary? Will Harley's former partner be driven by revenge or virtue? https://books2read.com/warbot

Other books by Billy DeCarlo:

Vigilante Angels Book I: The Priest

A former US Marine receives a terminal prognosis. But when a local priest is accused of molesting children, he hears the calling of another mission. He enlists a coterie of like-minded patients to seek his brand of justice. The hardest battles are right in his own home: an alcoholic, unfaithful wife and bringing himself to accept his son's sexuality. Will his fight against evil come too close to home? https://www.books2read.com/VigilanteAngelsBook1

Vigilante Angels Book II: The Cop

A dying vigilante finds himself under investigation by a racist, corrupt detective. When the detective crosses a line and involves family, the hunted decides becomes hunter. He partners with a one-eyed Korean martial arts expert and a black motorcycle gang to seek revenge. Will justice be served, and upon whom? https://www.books2read.com/VigilanteAngelsBook2

Vigilante Angels Book III: The Candidate

A terminally ill vigilante is on the run—quietly living out his last days in the Florida Keys. He manages to keep a low profile until love finds him and a hateful, divisive presidential candidate threatens to tear the country apart. As love and his desire to leave the world a better place pull at his heart, which will win? https://www.books2read.com/VigilanteAngelsBook3

ABOUT THE AUTHOR
Billy DeCarlo

Billy DeCarlo is an American author of novels and short stories.

A Note to My Readers

At my core, I'm a humble, blue-collar guy who has always loved to write. To be honest, I don't seek fame—perhaps just enough fortune to pay the bills. I write because I need to write.

The most rewarding thing a writer can receive is a review from those who enjoyed the work.

The most constructive thing a writer can receive is a private message with anything that can help to improve his or her work.

I do hope that you sign up for the newsletter at my website so that you hear about future books, editions, and other news.

Reviews are the currency of the craft. If you enjoyed my book, please take time to write a review.

Thank you and I hope you enjoyed this book!